The Viking at Drumshee

Drumshee Timeline Series
Book 9

Cora Harrison taught primary-school children in
England for twenty-five years before moving to a small
farm in Kilfenora, Co. Clare. The farm includes an Iron
Age fort, with the remains of a small castle inside it,
and the mysterious atmosphere of this ancient place
gave Cora the idea for a series of historical novels
tracing the survival of the ringfort through the
centuries. *The Viking at Drumshee* is Book 9 in the
Drumshee Timeline Series.

For Diarmuid O'Donoghue,
who has written lots of books himself
although he is only six years old

OTHER TITLES BY CORA HARRISON

The Viking at Drumshee

Drumshee Timeline Series
Book 9

Cora Harrison

WOLFHOUND PRESS
Celebrating 25 *Years*

First published in 2000 by
Wolfhound Press Ltd
68 Mountjoy Square
Dublin 1, Ireland
Tel: (353-1) 874 0354
Fax: (353-1) 872 0207

The Arts Council / An Chomhairle Ealaíon

Wolfhound Press receives financial assistance from The Arts Council/An Chomhairle Ealaíon, Dublin, Ireland.

British Library Cataloguing in Publication Data
A catalogue record for this book is available from the British Library.

ISBN 0-86327-788-8

10 9 8 7 6 5 4 3 2 1

Cover Illustration: Peter Gibson
Cover Design: Sally Mills-Westley
Line Drawing: Jeanette Dunne
Typesetting: Wolfhound Press
Printed in the UK by Cox & Wyman Ltd, Reading, Berks.

ChApter One

'**Watch** his left side! I'll guard his back.'

That was the first time Conn heard that terrible note of fear in his father's voice. For most of the battle, Patrick had seemed to be concentrating on keeping his fourteen-year-old son out of trouble, but now all that was swept aside. Prince Brian Boru, heir to his brother King Mahon of Thomand, and the great hope and hero of the Dalcassian tribe, was in such deadly danger that every man of the tribe, whether he was fourteen or forty, had to do his all to defend him.

On and on came the Vikings, the rain glinting on their iron helmets and dripping from the straight nose-pieces. It seemed impossible that the leather-clad, poorly armed Irish could beat them. Taller, much taller than the Irish, these Vikings seemed like giants, blond giants wielding their enormous two-handed axes, sweeping away all before them as they pressed on.

A short scream came from the Irishman in front of Brian, and he collapsed in a great fountain of blood. A Viking's battleaxe had split him down the middle from head to foot. Conn shuddered, but kept his eyes fixed unwaveringly ahead of him. Prince Brian is all that matters, he told himself; Father will guard his back, and I must keep anyone from getting too near his left side. Resolutely he took a firmer grip on his heavy spear and kept it moving ahead of him, creating a gap in the Viking ranks, through which Prince Brian moved as one with a charmed life.

Another Irishman went down, without even time for a scream. Surely now even Brian Boru himself would be forced to retreat.... But no: the mighty voice rose up, louder than any trumpet.

'Charge!' Brian Boru yelled, a thousand lights flashing from his sword as it split the raindrops.

'Charge!' echoed Conn, hearing with displeasure how thin and reedy his boy's voice sounded compared to the voice of his hero. It doesn't matter, he told himself severely; all that matters is fighting, and I can fight as well as any man.

'Brian *abú*!' came the response from the Irish warriors.

Just above Conn's head, a Viking battleaxe reared and began to descend. Without meaning to, Conn lowered his spear and watched, as if frozen, the mighty weapon coming nearer to his head.

And then it stopped. A bright sword had flashed, the battleaxe had fallen to the ground, and its owner's head rolled beside it.

'Keep your spear up, boy,' said Brian Boru, and his flashing sword sliced off yet another Viking head.

They were working in partnership now, Brian of Boru and Conn of Drumshee. It was as if they had trained to do this for months. Conn swept the great spear in wide semicircular movements, and when some Viking was unwise enough to try to push the annoyance aside, Brian Boru neatly sliced his head off. Behind them, Conn could hear his father grunt with effort as his sword stabbed into enemy bodies.

But still the Vikings came. There was no end to

them. There must have been five or six shiploads of them; they had come up the River Fergus from Limerick and fallen on Prince Brian's band of guerrilla warriors. The Vikings knew that they must kill Brian. If they killed him, his warriors would go back to King Mahon. King Mahon, childless, peace-loving and busy with his prayers, was no threat to them.

Thank God for the rain, thought Conn. The heavy black sky, full of rain-clouds, was bringing the October day to a close even earlier than usual. The Vikings wouldn't risk fighting once darkness fell. Brian Boru's troops knew this bleak countryside too well. For many weary months — ever since Prince Brian had quarrelled so bitterly with his brother, King Mahon — they had camped out here, fighting the roving bands of Vikings. They had had success, too — but they had paid for it: bit by bit, as warriors were killed by the Vikings or by disease and semi-starvation, their band had got smaller and smaller.

Now, perhaps, they were going to pay the ultimate price of their daring. This was no chance band of Vikings out to rob cattle or to plunder abbeys; this was a military force, sent out from Limerick to find the renowned Brian Boru and either kill him or bring him back to Limerick in chains.

But Brian Boru was not daunted. Still he pressed forward. Still he encouraged his remaining men onwards, through the mist and the rain.

Suddenly Conn understood. Brian Boru wasn't leading a fruitless last charge which would end in death for them all; he was luring the Vikings towards the precipice which overhung the eastern end of the lake. In the half-light, with the driving rain in their faces, the Vikings wouldn't see the steep cliff until it was too late. With renewed hope, Conn drove his heavy spear into the neck of the Viking in front of him and added his high, boyish voice to the deep, trumpet-like tones beside him.

Nearer and nearer to the precipice they came. Conn heard a triumphant note in his father's voice. He too must have guessed what Prince Brian was doing. The shouts of 'Boru!' rose above the war cries of the Vikings. The little band of desperate Irishmen had seen a glimmer of hope, although they were surrounded on all sides by the invaders from the far north.

Conn's heart was thumping, and his shoulder ached so much with the effort of holding up the heavy spear that he felt the pain all the way down his right side.

You must keep going! some voice in his mind screamed at him.

I can't, cried his exhausted body.

You can! replied the voice; and suddenly Conn knew that he could. He felt as if a goblet of mead, that intoxicating mixture of honey and herbs, were coursing through his veins. He broke into a run and, elbow to elbow with Brian Boru, drove the Vikings through the thick mist, through the approaching darkness — and over the rocky precipice. Sobbing for breath, he leaned on his spear and listened to the splashes as the broken bodies of the Vikings tumbled helplessly over the jagged rocks and fell into the icy waters of the lake below.

'The rest of them are retreating, my lord!' Patrick's exultant voice seemed to drive another draught of courage through Conn's veins. He stood a little straighter and looked at Prince Brian.

Brian looked the same as always, not even slightly out of breath. He smiled slightly at his shield-bearer.

'They've retreated,' he said wryly. 'But they haven't gone away. They'll be back.'

Conn looked around, and his heart sank. They had been left in possession of the field; but was this really all that was left of the band that had begun fighting that morning? He counted the men, and then counted again. There was no mistake. Brian Boru had only twenty warriors left, and of those twenty, one was a fourteen-year-old boy.

It was too much to hope that the rest of the Vikings would sail back to Limerick. They knew how many they had killed. As soon as light dawned, the Vikings would attack again, and this time there would be no mistake. Brian Boru and his men would be captured or killed.

'Best get some rest while we can,' said Brian, sinking down on the ground and wrapping his bratt, his cloak, around him.

The other men arranged themselves around him without a word. In the half-light, their faces were set in lines of despair.

Conn couldn't bear to look. Pulling his bratt around him, he stumbled away, his face wet with rain and tears. He stumbled on a small ring of rocks; even if they didn't shelter him from the thick rain, they would protect him from the worst of the wind. He wedged himself half under an overhanging boulder and buried his face in his knees.

It was the cold on his face that woke him. Soon after midnight, the rain must have ceased, and now the moon and all of the stars were brilliant in the black sky. Inside the thickness of Conn's wool bratt, his tunic had dried with the heat of his body, and only his face was cold.

Cautiously he got to his feet and looked around.

Prince Brian and all his men were still asleep. They should have left someone on guard, but the heavy rain had made this seem unnecessary. Apprehensively, Conn looked across the stony meadow to where the River Fergus gleamed in the silvery light of the moon. There were the Viking dragon-ships — six of them! The large square sail in the centre of each ship, the carved dragon-heads on each end, the lines of shields hung on the sides of the boats: every detail was as clear as in broad daylight.

With another quick glance at the sleeping men gathered around their leader, Conn began to creep forward, testing the uneven ground with each foot and taking care to make no noise.

Five of the ships were large ones — graceful, narrow shapes with carved heads on each end and a striped square-rigged sail in the centre of the ship. Those must be longships, Conn thought. He had heard Prince Brian describe the different boats to his father. The men slept on these. He could see their hump-backed shapes. They slept on the rowers' benches, their heads on their knees, or else stretched out on the aft deck. They had left no watchman, either. They didn't need to. They knew how few of the Irish warriors were left. At first dawn they would seize them. With the lake and a treacherous bog at their backs and the river in front of them, there would be no escape for the Irish.

The sixth boat, however, was empty. It was a small, shallow boat; it would probably be used in places where the water wasn't deep enough for the bigger longships. The Vikings continually sent out raiding parties to seize cattle for food and even women and children for slaves. This boat could be beached anywhere. It was moored a little way from the others.

Carefully Conn looked around. There was no movement from the sleeping Vikings. He would be able to get close enough to examine the small boat and see how it was built.

The water of the River Fergus was very clear, and Conn could see down to its sandy bottom. To his surprise, the boat was not flat underneath. He had never seen a boat like it. The few boats he had known were circular and flat-bottomed, but the bottom of this boat slanted to make a knife-like edge to cut through the water. So this is how they go so fast, thought Conn.

At that instant, his hair was seized, his head was jerked back and a short sword flashed in front of his dazzled eyes.

For a moment, blinded by the light reflecting off the weapon, Conn closed his eyes and waited for the massive two-handed axe to descend and cut off his short life for ever. His heart gave one mighty thump....

Then he opened his eyes again, and hope began to flow back into him. This was no massive axe, but a short sword such as he himself had often worn — a boy's weapon, he thought contemptuously. At the same instant, he realised that the Viking who held him was no giant, but a boy of his age, or thereabouts. He was taller than Conn, but his face was beardless and the hand that held Conn's hair seemed to lack power.

With a quick jerk, Conn spun around and drove his knee into the Viking boy's groin, and heard him gasp. The fight became vicious. The sword made contact with Conn's shoulder, and he felt blood warm against his neck. His hand fumbled for his own sword, but the thick folds of his bratt made it difficult; he abandoned the attempt and relied on his fists and his teeth and his lightly shod feet, kicking and punching. The Viking boy rocked backwards and then came on again with a quick rush. The point of his sword lunged against Conn's breast, but there was no force behind it and the thick leather tunic easily turned the blow away.

The boy was tiring. His breath came in quick, short gasps. Why hasn't he called for help? thought Conn, and that very thought lent strength to his arm as, in a last desperate attempt to save his life, he lashed out with his fist and struck the boy on the chin. The boy dropped to the ground like a felled ox.

Quickly Conn snatched up the dropped sword and stood over the Viking boy, pointing the sword at his heart. But there was no need. For the moment, the boy was unconscious.

Conn bent over him. His breathing was strong and even. Soon he would regain consciousness, and the first thing he would do would surely be to call for help.

With fingers which shook a little in spite of all his attempts to hold them steady, Conn unwound the belt around his tunic. His mother had woven it for him from the finest, softest wool, just before he had gone off with his father. He hated to spoil it, but he had to gag this Viking quickly. He pulled the boy's mouth open, stuffed some of the belt in behind the strong white teeth, and tied it around the boy's head. With his dagger, he cut off a length of the belt and tied the boy's hands behind his back. Then, with a cautious eye on the dragon-ships rocking peacefully on the broad waters of the Fergus, he shook the boy by the shoulder.

After a minute, large pale-blue eyes opened and the boy shook his head slightly. He's all right, thought Conn. He doesn't even look dizzy. He can walk.

With the point of the sword, he jabbed the boy and indicated to him to get up. The boy stood up and glanced at the small boat, as if measuring the distance between it and him.

Conn lifted the sword and held the point against the boy's throat. 'Walk,' he whispered.

It seemed as if the Viking boy understood: he shrugged his shoulders and began to walk steadily, almost indifferently, just ahead of Conn.

Chapter Two

Conn had left a sleeping camp, but he returned to one that was alert and awake. The moonlight had woken everyone, and his absence had been discovered. For a moment Conn saw a look of terrible anxiety on his father's face; then it was replaced by relief, anger and finally disbelief.

'What in God's name have you there?' Patrick demanded, his low voice thick with suppressed anger.

'I've captured a slave,' replied Conn, taking care to whisper, but pride broke through and made his voice squeak a little on the last word. He gave the Viking boy a slight shake to restore his dignity.

'Oh God, give me patience,' prayed his father. All the men around grinned, and Prince Brian threw back his head and laughed, soundlessly, but with real enjoyment.

'Well, why not?' persisted Conn sullenly. 'He could be useful. We could use him as a bargaining tool if the worst comes.'

'The worst will come,' said Brian gravely. 'This moon is so bright that it must waken the Vikings soon. They won't wait until daylight.'

Conn looked around him. The moon was extraordinarily bright, casting shadows everywhere like a noonday sun. In the middle of the bog, a wind-torn tree cast a black-etched shadow on the ground. It looks like a banshee, he thought.

And then a memory came to him. He hadn't thought of this image; someone else had said it. It had been Emer, his sister. Conn shook his head, trying to dispel the mists of tiredness inside his mind, but it was no good; it was definitely Emer who had called it a 'banshee tree'. He frowned with puzzlement. How could Emer know this tree? he thought. She's not here.

He looked again at the tree. The persistent west wind had moulded it so that all the twiggy branches were swept to one side; it did indeed look like the hair of a fairy woman streaming out in the wind.

And then he remembered. Yes, Emer had said it. She had been there, at that spot, with him. They had stolen away one summer day, found a trackway through the bog and gone fishing there at the lake.

'Father,' he said, so urgently that he forgot to whisper, 'I know a way out of here. I know how to cross the bog. As long as I can see that tree, I can cross it safely.'

'Keep your voice down,' hissed his father. 'You don't know what you're talking about. Everyone knows that bog is impassable. Even the Vikings know it. That's why they've left us sitting here, like wolves in a trap.'

'Let the boy speak.' Brian's deep voice was so low that it carried less than a whisper would have. 'Conn fought like a man yesterday. Today we must listen to him as we would to any man.'

Conn drew a deep breath. Suddenly he knew how he could save the remainder of Prince Brian Boru's gallant army. He had the whole plan worked out in his head. He had to explain it so well that he would convince the men.

'My lord,' he said steadily, adopting Brian's deep, quiet voice as nearly as he could, 'one day, two summers ago, my sister and I found a path through the bog. We wanted to go fishing, but it was too far to go around by the valley, so we took bundles of willow sticks and probed the ground before every footstep, and we found our way across. We left the sticks standing there so that we could find our way back.'

There was a movement of anger from Patrick. There'll be trouble afterwards, Conn thought. Emer was their father's darling, and he would be blamed bitterly for having taken her into such danger. However, that wasn't important now. Deliberately Conn turned his back on his father and faced Prince Brian, looking squarely into the hazel eyes.

'When we were going back, we discovered that, if we kept the tree in line with that big eagle-shaped rock up there on the cliff, we would stay on the path. It's quite a wide path. We were in no danger of falling off if we kept those two things lined up.'

'And what then? Is there somewhere at the other side of the bog where we could stay, somewhere to keep ourselves safe from the Vikings, to heal our wounded and build up our strength?'

The prince is near to despair, thought Conn. He could hear it in the deep voice. He gathered up all his resources, and when he spoke his voice was quick and eager.

'You could come back with us to our fort at Drumshee.' He turned and included his father in his glance. Patrick looked startled, but there was a glint of dawning hope in his eye.

'It's not very far from here to Drumshee, if you go across the bog. Emer and I walked it in a couple of hours. You'd be safe there. There's a secret place, an underground room, right in the centre of the fort. We have a great wall all around the fort, and gardens for pot herbs, and the forests of Kylemore are full of deer. You could spend the winter there — build up strength, recruit more men.'

Conn stopped. He had run out of breath. The effort of communicating his enthusiasm while keeping his voice low and almost soundless in that still, frosty air was almost too much for him. He looked at his father, but Patrick had his eyes fixed on Prince Brian. Conn turned his eyes back to that stern, bearded face. The decision was Brian's.

There was a moment's silence; then Brian got to his feet briskly.

'What are we waiting for?' he asked. 'This way, there's a chance. If we stay here, there is none. You lead the way, boy; we'll follow and trust to you. Do your best, and the rest is in the hands of God.'

'What about the Viking boy?' asked Patrick.

'Put a dagger in his throat,' said one of the men. 'No sense in leaving him here to tell them where we've gone and set them on our trail. He's heard us talking, too. Some of these Vikings know some Irish. I think he does. I watched him while you were talking.'

Conn looked at the boy. The man was right: he should be killed. There was no sense in leaving him behind, and to take an unwilling captive along the dangerous path was asking for trouble.

He hesitated, looking at the Viking boy. He did understand Irish; there was no doubt about that. The pale-blue eyes were full of fear. In an instant, Conn made up his mind.

'No,' he said roughly. 'He's my captive. I'm not

leaving him behind. I want him for a body servant.'

Before anyone could say anything else, he snatched up a rope, tied it around the Viking boy's wrists, put the free end over his own shoulder and set off at a trot towards the path through the bog.

It was a dreadful responsibility. For a moment, Conn wavered. The path had looked very different on that sunny summer day when he and Emer had crossed it. He remembered all the flowers that had been growing there, and how Emer had noticed bog cotton growing in the wettest spots. Now the whole path and the treacherous bog alike were black in the moonlight.

Conn half-turned. I shouldn't take this responsibility, he thought. It was up to the men, up to Prince Brian, to lead them out of this deadly danger.

'Carry on,' said Brian's deep, quiet voice. 'We're right behind you. We'll trust you and follow in your footsteps.'

Conn still hesitated; and then the moonlight showed him the face of his captive. There was almost a smile in the pale-blue eyes. The boy knew that Conn was afraid, that he wanted to go back. With a savage jerk of the rope, Conn turned his face back towards the banshee tree and strode on.

Keep the eagle rock above the banshee tree, he whispered to himself, saying the words over and over again as if they were a prayer or a magic charm. The path was very wet beneath its light crust of frost. The mud squelched beneath his feet and oozed over his sandals, but the path held firm.

Conn was becoming more confident. Keeping the tree and the rock firmly in his sight-lines, he broke into a slow trot. Behind him, the Viking boy also trotted, the rope slack and easy between them.

'Well done, boy; that's a good path,' said Brian Boru from behind him. Conn glowed at the praise. He cast a worried glance upwards. The weather here in the west of Ireland could change in a matter of moments, and if clouds came over the moon, they would have to stop; he needed to see his two marks plainly. However, the moon still shone silver in the starlit sky. No worries there, he thought. There wasn't a cloud in the sky. They might even get across the bog before day broke.

Once more he quickened his pace — but the next minute, the rope over his shoulder jerked, grew taut and scraped against his neck, his feet skidded from under him and he fell flat on his back.

'What in the name of thunder do you think you're doing?' he muttered savagely as he scrambled to his feet. The fall had hurt his back and, worse still, upset his dignity. Had that Viking boy done it on purpose? Conn felt like hitting him.

But then he stopped. The boy was looking not at him, but back over his shoulder. His mouth was still stuffed with the gag, but he turned, looked hard at Conn and then jerked his head towards the river.

Now Conn understood. In the quietness of the night he could barely hear the noise, but it was un-mistakable. It was the sound of water splashing off the ends of oars. The Vikings were coming. Quite soon, their absence would be discovered.

Conn looked around desperately. The moon was still bright. As soon as the Vikings landed, they would see Brian Boru's band, and the path they had taken across the bog would be fairly clear. If only we were just a little further on! he thought. Then we'd have been opposite the Viking landing-place, but the Vikings wouldn't have realised that the path cuts diagonally across the bog. If they'd tried to go directly across at that spot, they'd have sunk.

There was only one thing to do. They would have to keep down low. Quickly Conn took out his dagger and approached the Viking boy. He could see the fear in the boy's eyes, but there was no time for explanations. With one quick slash, he cut the rope that bound the boy's wrists; in a hoarse whisper, he said, 'Get down on your hands and knees, everyone; we'll have to crawl until we get to that clump of bilberry bushes.'

Once we're past there, he thought, we'll be directly opposite the Viking landing-place, but well out of range of their throwing-spears. Then it'll be safe to stand up and show ourselves.

He didn't spare a glance for the Viking boy. At least he had a chance now; he could use his hands and crawl with the others. If he had any sense, he would see that it would be better to stay with Conn than to risk his life in the treacherous bog.

The crawl to the bilberry bushes seemed agonisingly slow. Conn heard the Viking boy, behind him, cough and spit. Of course, now that his hands were free, he had rid himself of the gag. He made no sound, however, just followed close on Conn's heels.

There was no sound from the Viking warriors, either — not even the sound of their oars on the water. They must have landed, Conn thought. He pictured them advancing silently, hoping to surprise a sleeping camp of Irishmen. His nerves were so on edge that he felt as if he would scream, but he knew that his plan was a good one.

Grabbing one of the Viking boy's wrists and hauling his captive in front of him, he got to his feet and boldly faced the Viking battle force.

In spite of the blond-haired human shield which he held in front of him, one or two Vikings hurled their throwing-spears at him; but, as he had guessed, the distance was too great and the spears landed in the bog. Conn fixed his eyes on them. He had wagered everything on the chance that the path he had taken was the only dry, firm track through the bog. For a moment, he wasn't sure; but then the spears began to sink, and before the rest of the Irish band had joined him on the path beyond the bilberry bushes, only the hilts were visible through the dark moss.

'Keep walking, everyone,' said Prince Brian. 'Walk, and look frightened.'

He's guessed, thought Conn exultantly. He's guessed what I want to do!

With some bewildered glances back, the rest of the party followed. The Vikings sent up a great yell of exultation and charged across the treacherous bog.

Conn stopped. Nothing could have moved him at that moment. His plan had worked! No sooner were the first Vikings on the bog than their battle-cries turned to cries for help; and then the whole scene turned into utter chaos, with men sinking and other men throwing themselves flat on the turf to pull them out.

'Come,' said Brian Boru. 'Let's make our way while we still have light to do it.'

With a start, Conn looked up at the sky. Clouds had appeared from nowhere and were scudding across the moon. If they didn't reach the banshee tree soon, they too would be swallowed up by the bog.

Chapter Three

This is like a nightmare, thought Conn; like one of those nightmares where you know it's going to get unbearable soon, and you madly struggle to wake yourself. He had led them into a trap — his father, all the Irish band, and above all Prince Brian, the Kingdom of Thomand's only hope of defeating the Vikings who terrorised and laid waste the land of Ireland.

They stood close to one another, every man fearing to move a step, while around them the rain fell and the moon was barely a lighter shade of navy beneath the heavy clouds. They were unable to see even the white faces of their friends; there was no hope whatsoever of seeing the banshee-shaped tree or the eagle-shaped rock.

'We'll have to wait until dawn,' said Brian Boru. 'We'll be able to cross the rest of the bog then.'

Yes, thought Conn, but at dawn the Vikings will see what we're doing, and they'll be able to send their men around the lake and through the valley at the far side. If only we could cross by night, they would never know which way we're going....

Cautiously he moved one foot, sliding it along the wet mud and then pressing, at first gently, then shifting his whole weight onto it. It held. He moved his other foot, again sliding it until he felt firm ground under it. Then the right foot again. He was definitely on the path.

Hope began to rise in him. Perhaps by some instinct he was still going the correct way, keeping to the right path. Excitedly he moved his other foot. The ground felt springy now, but still firm enough to hold his weight. As long as I keep my face towards the breeze I should be all right, he thought.

The next minute he was sinking into the soft, wet, fibrous mud.

Conn struggled frantically, but silently. He wouldn't risk anyone else's life because of his own stupidity, he vowed. Brian Boru had trusted him, and he had behaved like an impatient child.

He was deep in the mud, up to his knees now, but he was still able to do what he should have done at once. He threw himself backwards onto the bog, spreading his arms as wide as he could and praying that it would hold his weight.

His back and head remained above ground. That was more than he had dared to hope for. Now he had to gradually pull his legs clear. With all his strength, he tried to raise his right leg. It made a squelching sound, but he couldn't free it, and his efforts drove his back deeper into the soggy mess. He didn't dare try that again, or even his head would soon be under the bog. At the thought of the slow death by suffocation which awaited him, he sucked in his breath in a suppressed sob of agony.

It was then, when he had ceased to hope, that he heard a whisper. It was a strange voice, a strange accent. He hardly understood it at first.

'Say your name,' said the voice.

'Conn,' he whispered back.

The next moment something struck him on the face, something hard, something wet from trailing in the mud. It was a rope. With the instinct of despair, he seized it and gripped it in both hands.

'Conn is in the bog,' whispered the strange voice. 'Hold on to me. He's on the end of my rope.'

Conn strained his ears to listen. No one said a word, but through the darkness he heard the sound of shuffling feet. They would be forming themselves into a human chain, he guessed. He braced himself for the first pull, but when it came it almost jerked his arms from their sockets. Grimly he held the end of the rope, feeling as if his body was being torn in two. Inch by inch, he was being dragged out of the bog, but it was agonisingly slow. His back felt as if it was being broken.

Still the thick mud of the bog held on to him. He would have to do something to help himself. Arching his back and exerting terrific pressure on his shoulders, he raised his hips with a convulsive movement. That helped; he felt himself move — only a few extra inches, but he couldn't be far from the path.

He lay for a moment with his eyes closed; then, gathering up all his strength, he gave another violent jerk. He felt the rope pulled strongly — and then he was out, lying on the solid path, his breath coming in great gasps. To his fury, he could hear his teeth chattering violently, and he despised himself, because he knew it was terror, not cold, that was making him shake all over like a trembling child.

'Get him out of those wet clothes,' said Brian Boru. 'Here, wrap my bratt around him. I don't need it.'

'He can have my bratt,' said the Viking boy. 'I'm his size. I'm not cold either.'

'Thanks,' said Conn awkwardly.

'Stand still,' whispered his father, stripping him

down and rubbing him dry with a corner of his own bratt. He handled his son roughly, shaking him and almost rubbing his skin off.

I suppose he's furious with me, thought Conn ruefully. But then, as his father finished drying him with a quick rub of his back — a rub which was almost a caress — he realised how frightened Patrick had been, and how thankful he was that his son was still alive.

Conn reached out and squeezed his father's wrist. 'Sorry,' he muttered, wondering whether he should apologise to Prince Brian as well.

'Let's sit down,' said Prince Brian, before Conn could say anything. 'Sit, and link hands with your neighbours. That way no one will be lost.'

Conn sat down with instant obedience. From now on I'm going to follow orders, he thought. On his left side, he could feel his father. He reached out and clutched his hand, and it relieved his feeling of shame when Patrick squeezed his hand in return.

On Conn's right, a hand found his. It was a smaller hand than his father's; a boy's hand. Cautiously, still holding the hand, Conn felt the owner's tunic. That boy would get cold, sitting on the soaking-wet ground without a bratt around him. Conn let go of the hand, arranged the bratt around both of their shoulders, and leaned towards the boy to share his warmth with him.

'How did you learn to speak Irish?' he whispered.

'My mother was Irish,' the boy whispered back.

'Oh.' Conn was startled. He hadn't expected that. 'Is your father Irish?' he asked.

'No, he is Viking.'

'Oh,' said Conn again. He didn't like to ask any

questions about the Viking father. Perhaps he was dead. The boy's voice sounded funny. (Of course, Conn thought, it might be just that his voice is breaking, like mine. We must be about the same age.) Conn supposed that the boy's mother was probably a bondswoman, a slave, captured by the Vikings on their raids.

A great wave of rage came over him. I'll fight with Brian Boru until the last Viking is driven out of Ireland, he vowed silently. He felt a sudden pity for the half-Viking boy. Perhaps he wouldn't really have him for a slave; perhaps they might even be friends.

'What's your name?' he whispered.

'Ivar,' replied the boy.

'Ivar,' repeated Conn. It was a Viking name. There had been a King Ivar. At least it was easy to say, though.

'Where do you live, Ivar?'

'Near Limerick.' Ivar turned away. Conn felt him move, and felt a back where there had been a shoulder. I'd better not ask him any more questions, thought Conn. He doesn't really want to talk about his home.

In any case, Conn was feeling sleepy. His head drooped, then jerked suddenly as Ivar prodded him.

'Look,' said Ivar. 'The rain stops.'

Conn looked up at the sky. There was still no sign of the moon, but the sky was definitely growing lighter; it had turned dark blue, with a sheen of silver beneath. He kept his eyes steadily fixed on the silvery bit. It broadened, became more definite, and the large silver circle of the moon began to burn off the clouds.

What a fool I was! thought Conn. If only I had

waited for another five minutes.... He shrugged his shoulders and pushed the thought back. It was up to him to lead the last remnants of Brian Boru's army to the safety of Drumshee.

Silently he touched his father's arm and pointed to the moon. In a minute all of the men were on their feet. Carefully Conn lined up the banshee tree with the eagle rock and began to move steadily forward.

It was another half-hour before they reached the tree. They stopped for a moment and looked back.

'See — the glint of the moonlight on Viking armour,' said Prince Brian in a low voice. 'We can see them, but they won't see us.'

Conn looked around at the bedraggled band. It was true. The wet leather and dun-coloured bratts worn by the Irish were the same colour as the bog which surrounded them. Each man wore a hood pulled well over his face. The Vikings wouldn't see them. Another few yards and they would be safely across the bog, heading across the hilly moorland towards the ancient fort of Drumshee.

'This next stretch is the difficult bit,' he explained to his father in a low voice. 'When Emer and I came back, the willow sticks were still in place. It only seemed like a few steps then, but I think it might be about fifty yards.'

'Enough to drown a man,' said Patrick grimly. 'I'll do it first, and if it's safe the rest of you can follow.'

Conn opened his mouth to protest. It would obviously be easier for a boy's light weight to make that crossing in safety. In any case, he thought indignantly, I'm the leader of this journey.

And then, suddenly, something caught his eye. Just beyond the banshee tree was a smaller tree, only about a yard high; it was leafless, but the pointed shape of the tightly shut buds was enough for Conn. Hardly daring to hope, he moved cautiously forward and bent down to examine the little tree. There was no doubt about it: it was definitely a willow tree. It must have grown from one of the sticks that he and Emer had stuck in the ground two summers before.

He looked ahead of him, towards the eagle rock, but he could see nothing else, just flat vegetation. He looked to his right, and excitement welled up in him.

'Look!' he said, forgetting to whisper. 'Look — there are some of the sticks Emer and I put in the bog. The ground's drier here, and they took root. I know the way to dry land now.'

'You lead and we'll follow,' said Brian Boru. 'Let every man bend low and keep his face hidden in his hood. With God's help, we'll be at Drumshee by dawn.'

Chapter Four

Prince Brian was right. Dawn was just breaking when they climbed the steep hill to the fort at Drumshee. The whole kin-group turned out of their little thatched houses to see the ragged band of men and the famous Brian Boru, brother of the king. Conn's mother, Ita, ran to hug her husband, and Emer, Conn's sister, jumped into her father's arms. Then they both welcomed Prince Brian, and all the soaked and half-starved men were brought in to the fireside to be warmed and fed.

'You're welcome! You're very welcome!' said Cormac, Patrick's eldest brother, bustling in, as usual filling the room with his huge bulk and his booming voice. Cormac was a farmer and a blacksmith, two very profitable trades, and he always had an air of valuing himself very highly. Behind him was Flann, his thirteen-year-old son.

'Go on, Flann,' Cormac added, nudging his son in the ribs. 'Greet Prince Brian and tell him he's welcome to Drumshee.'

Flann muttered something. No one heard him and no one took much notice of him. No one ever took much notice of Flann. His father had already forgotten him and was helping himself to a cup of mead.

'Wait till I tell you what it was like,' whispered Conn to his cousin. 'There was blood everywhere. You can still smell it on my jerkin.'

Flann took a step back from Conn and went slightly green. Conn smirked with satisfaction. He knew that Flann hated blood. He was small and thin for his age, too, and Conn could never resist teasing him on every possible occasion.

'Leave the boy alone,' hissed Deirdre, Cormac's wife. Conn's mother had told her a hundred times that she spoiled Flann. 'He'll never grow up to be a man if you run to him every time he gets the slightest cut,' Ita had warned again and again, and it looked as if she had been right. Everyone laughed at Flann; even his own father was ashamed of him.

Conn moved away, still smirking, and went to greet his other uncle, Niall the wheelwright, and his wife and young children. Soon the little house was crammed full of people, and the level of the voices rose higher and higher.

'We'll have to move Prince Brian and the other men into the underground room within an hour,' said Patrick to his wife in a low voice. 'The Vikings might have followed our trail here, though I think the rain should have washed all our tracks away. We didn't see many people on our way — and I would swear that none of those we saw would ever betray us. Still, better be sure. We don't want any talk in the neighbourhood about strangers at Drumshee.'

'Don't you worry about that,' said Ita. She was bustling around, ladling food out of the big iron pot which hung over the fire and filling horn mugs with mead. 'Emer and I and your sisters will soon have everything ready for them down there. The men can help once they've rested.'

Emer was shy of Ivar. Funnily enough, thought Conn, she seemed to be more at ease with Brian Boru and all the rough, wild-looking men from his army.

'He's very good-looking,' she whispered to Conn, when they were dragging bales of oat straw down to the underground room.

'Who? Prince Brian?' asked Conn, purposely mis-understanding.

'No, stupid! I mean the Viking boy.'

'Oh, him,' said Conn loftily. 'I haven't really looked at him. He's just my body servant.'

'Stop showing off,' said Emer sharply. 'And stop pretending to be grown-up. You're only a year older than me.'

'Hurry up, you two,' shouted their mother. 'Are those beds ready yet?'

'What's his name?' asked Emer. Then she realised that the Viking boy had stopped on the steps down to the underground room and was looking back at her.

'Do you understand Irish?' she asked hastily, blushing slightly.

'Yes,' said the boy. 'My name is Ivar.' He smiled and added, 'My mother looks like you. She has black hair and blue eyes too.'

'Oh,' said Emer.

She sounds startled, Conn thought. 'Ivar's mother is Irish,' he explained in a low voice, as Ivar went ahead of them into the underground room. 'His father is a Viking.' Again the desire to show off rose in him, and he added, 'He'll make a good slave, don't you think? I'll lend him to you, if you have any tasks that are too difficult for you. He's not too bad, though he's not as strong as I am.'

'You're very mean,' hissed Emer, pushing him so hard that he almost overbalanced. He tripped on the last step and arrived in the underground room in an awkward heap of arms and legs. The Viking boy turned around and laughed.

Conn picked himself sullenly. He wasn't hurt — he had fallen on a heap of oat straw — but his dignity was upset. A couple of hours ago, he had been the hero of Prince Brian Boru's army, and now he had been pushed over by his sister, who was a year younger than he was. Furiously he launched himself at Ivar's grinning face.

Emer gave them one glance and then ran back up the stone-flagged steps, screaming, 'Father, Conn is killing the Viking boy!'

To her slight embarrassment, it was Prince Brian who came out of the round thatched house. He was yawning slightly and wiping his mouth.

'Where are they?' he asked, sounding amused.

'Down in the underground room,' replied Emer. 'Quick! Conn is very strong — he'll kill that poor boy. He's half-Irish, too.'

Without looking to see whether he followed, she led the way, running confidently down the steps and bursting into the underground room.

'Stop it, Conn!' she screamed. 'Stop it! Prince Brian is coming.'

That had an effect, she was pleased to see. Conn lowered his fists and turned around, startled, and Ivar quickly got a blow in, so that by the time Prince Brian reached the bottom of the steps both boys were bleeding.

He looked at them in silence for a minute and then said quietly, 'Save your fighting for the real enemy, Conn. No man in my army mistreats someone weaker than himself.'

Conn flushed. But he looks quite pleased, really,

thought Emer. He's flattered that Prince Brian has noticed how strong he is.

Brian Boru turned to Ivar. 'Emer tells me you're half-Irish. Is that true?'

'Yes, my lord,' said Ivar stiffly. 'My mother is Irish.'

'In that case, you might wish to join us. Would your mother want you to?'

'Yes, my lord,' repeated Ivar, just as woodenly. Then a flash of fire came into his pale-blue eyes and he added, 'My mother hates the Vikings. She weeps for her kin and her birthplace.'

Brian Boru patted him on the back. 'In that case, you will fight with us, and if we get a chance, we'll rescue your mother. Conn will train you. He's a good fighter.'

Emer looked at Conn dubiously. It sounded as if Ivar wouldn't be Conn's slave after all. How would Conn like that?

Conn, however, was looking very pleased at the praise. He had drawn himself up to look as tall as possible.

'Yes, my lord,' he said. 'I'll teach him everything I know.'

'I can teach you things, too,' said Ivar stubbornly.

Emer groaned to herself. She looked at Prince Brian and smiled. 'Boys are so difficult, aren't they?' she said, in her most grown-up fashion. 'I don't know why they always have to be quarrelling all the time.'

'I was the same at their age,' Prince Brian assured her. 'It's a waste of energy, though,' he went on hastily. 'We need to train and train so that we'll be ready to fight the Vikings.'

'Were you fighting the Vikings when you were my age?' asked Conn shyly.

'No,' said Brian with a sigh. 'No one allowed me to fight. I was a younger son. I was sent off to a monastery to study. I was older than you when I came to join my brother, who had just been made king. I would have preferred to stay with him and fight. I've always hated the Vikings, ever since they attacked our fort at Boru and killed my mother and my brothers. I was only seven years old then, but I never forgot.'

He had the look of someone who wanted to banish unpleasant memories. Conn remembered his father telling him that Prince Brian and his brother King Mahon had disagreed, and that that was why Prince Brian had moved away and taken his band of warriors with him. He would have loved to ask how Prince Brian had become the greatest soldier ever known, but he knew that he had better say no more. Awkwardly he began to pile up the straw that he and Ivar had scattered during their fight.

Prince Brian looked around. 'Well, everything looks cosy,' he said. 'I'd better be getting my men down here. We don't want any talk about us for a while, until that party of Vikings goes back to Limerick. We'll have to keep a man on the lookout all the time. If the Vikings think we're here, they'll burn everything. Now remember, Conn: don't fight. As Ivar says, he can teach you something, and you can teach him.'

He went back up the steps.

Conn looked at Ivar challengingly. 'What could you teach me, anyway?' he asked, with a sneer in his voice.

The Viking boy looked at him steadily. 'I could teach you to build a boat,' he said. 'How would you like that?'

Conn caught his breath. In his mind's eye he could see those magnificent boats. He would have given anything to own one of those, with the knife-like bottom that could cleave through the water like a knife.

He looked at Ivar. 'You couldn't!' he jeered. 'You're only a boy. I bet you know nothing about it.'

Ivar shrugged. 'Please yourself,' he said. He sat down on one of the bales of oat straw and mopped his face with a handful of straw.

Conn watched him in silence for a moment, but the temptation was too great.

'Could you really show me how to build a boat?' he asked.

'Yes,' said Ivar briefly.

Conn waited, but Ivar said no more and Conn was forced to go on.

'How do you know how to build a boat?'

'My father taught me,' said Ivar. 'He is a boat-builder. If you have wood, we can build a boat.'

Conn waited. He's dying to know more, thought Emer, but he doesn't want to ask.

'Tell us about it, Ivar,' she said quickly. 'How did your father teach you to build boats?'

'I had to start by building a small boat,' said Ivar readily, 'a boat not much bigger than my foot. I had to make it so that it would sail well and not let in water. I made boat after boat, and I used to take them down to the river and try them out.'

He stopped, his face clouding over and his pale-blue eyes turning the icy colour that they had when he was angry.

'Go on,' said Emer. 'Tell us about it.'

'Oh, shut up pestering,' said Conn roughly. He

was disturbed by something in Ivar's face — a look of anger, even of hate.

'No,' said Ivar, after a short struggle with himself. 'I'll tell you. It doesn't matter now. I made boat after boat, and then, when I'd made one that I thought was really good, I asked my father to come and see it. I made a little sail with cloth that my mother gave me, striped cloth, and I tied a piece of string to the prow of the boat and let it sail down the river with the wind behind it.'

'And what did your father say?' asked Emer gently. He didn't really want to tell, she knew that, but he would feel better when he had told someone. She saw tears well up in his eyes, and she put her hand over his comfortingly.

'Well, he didn't say anything until I took the boat out. Then he held out his hand. I put the boat into his hand, and he ... he ... he threw it into the middle of the river. The last I saw of it, it was sailing down towards the sea.'

There was a silence. Imagine if my father was like that, thought Conn. He remembered Patrick making his first sword for him. He had made it out of wood, and he had made himself a wooden sword as well, with a leather cover over the tip of it. Together they had practised swordplay for hours on end. Conn remembered how Patrick had called Ita to look, and how proud he had been, and how he had praised his son. Poor Ivar had nothing like that.

Conn tried to think of something to say, but he couldn't. He looked at Emer appealingly, and she understood.

'That was really mean and horrible of your father,' she said hotly. 'Did you go on making boats?'

Ivar nodded. 'Yes, I did,' he said. 'For a day or two I thought I would never make another boat, but my mother persuaded me to carry on. She told me that my father had thrown my boat away because he wanted me to do better, because he wanted me to be as good a boat-builder as himself. She ... she came down and looked at my boats, and she told me what was wrong. She had learned a lot from my father because she used to hold pieces of wood for him. I didn't show them to my father any more, though. But I helped him in his workshop, and once when he was sick I finished a boat, and when it was launched, everyone said it was the best boat he had ever made. He never said that I had made more than half of it, though, and he never praised me for it.'

'But you'll teach us, won't you?' asked Emer, quite excited at the thought of a little boat. 'We can sail them down the River Fergus. It's just down there at the bottom of the hill. Make friends with him, Conn. You know Prince Brian told you to.'

'Friends,' said Conn with a grin, holding out his hand to Ivar.

'Friends,' replied Ivar, his blue eyes lighting up and becoming warm again.

Chapter Five

Two days later, when everyone was rested and all the wounds had been doctored, Patrick suggested to Prince Brian that the whole party go hunting in the great forest of Kylemore. Already the stocks of meat were running low, with all the extra men to feed, and a few deer would make sure that there was plenty for all.

Luckily, Drumshee had plenty of the tall, sturdy ponies of the west of Ireland. Patrick bred them for sale at the fairs, and he had built up the stocks so that they could be sold at the fair at Samhain, at the end of October; there were enough ponies for all the men and for the three boys.

Conn had looked forward to teaching Ivar how to ride, but he was disappointed: the Viking boy jumped onto his pony with one bound and seemed better at horsemanship than Conn himself. Conn felt irritated. His eye fell on Flann, who was reluctantly pulling himself up onto his pony's back.

'It's going to be great, Flann,' he said wickedly. 'When we kill a deer, we slit him down the middle and take out all his insides, and all his blood floods out, and then....'

Flann slid rapidly off the pony and dashed behind the house with his hand firmly clamped over his mouth. Deirdre came running out of the house and followed him, her motherly clucking clearly audible to all the waiting men. Cormac flushed a dark red, and his mouth clamped in a tight line when his wife reappeared a few minutes later.

'Flann can't go with you,' she said firmly. 'He's not well.'

Cormac was speechless. The rest of the men looked embarrassed. Conn winked at Ivar, and Ita turned her eyes to heaven and heaved a sigh. 'Put the pony away, Emer,' she said.

'Oh, may I go?' asked Emer pleadingly. 'There's a spare pony now. Please? I'd love to go to Kylemore Forest.'

It was Ita's turn to be annoyed. 'No, you can't go,' she snapped. 'Stay here and help me with the washing. Stop trying to be a boy all the time.'

'Let her go,' said Cormac unexpectedly. 'I'm glad some of the young ones have some spirit.' He glared vindictively at his wife and gave the signal to everyone to start.

Emer gave a swift glance at her father. He always obeyed his elder brother, she knew that; but what would her mother say?

Quickly she turned to Prince Brian. 'Please, may I go?' she said. 'I'll remember for the rest of my life that I went hunting with Prince Brian Boru in the forest of Kylemore.'

He laughed at that — she had known he would — and turned to her mother. 'Let her go, Ita,' he said. 'Patrick and I will take good care of her. There's no danger.'

Ita smiled. 'Well, you behave yourself and do what you're told,' she said severely; but Emer knew that her mother was only pretending to be cross. She was flattered that Prince Brian was taking an interest in her children, and really she was quite proud of how adventurous and brave both Conn and Emer were, especially compared with Flann, the only other child of their age in the settlement at Drumshee.

It was a beautiful October day. The leaves in the forest were beginning to turn from green to shades of yellow and brown, and the air was sharp with a hint of frost. There were no signs of deer near the edge of the forest, though. Too many settlements were grouped around there, and the deer had retreated to the safety of the deep centre of Kylemore.

'We'll just keep riding towards the south, my lord,' said Cormac to Prince Brian. 'We'll meet them after an hour or two more. I'm sure of that. This forest is full of deer.'

'I know this place,' said Ivar to Emer, when they reached a clearing in the forest. 'At least, I think I do. Look at that old oak over there, that one that's been struck by lightning. We were here when that happened; we'd come deep into the forest because my father needed a tall, straight oak for the keel of a very large ship. Look, you can still see the tracks here where the tree was dragged. All the men of the settlement helped to bring it back. That was the biggest ship we'd ever made. It was thirty paces long.'

'Do you miss your home?' asked Emer timidly. She couldn't quite make out the expression on his face. It could have been sadness, or anger; she wasn't sure which.

'No,' said Ivar abruptly. Then he turned to her. 'Don't tell anyone what I said. Promise me.'

'I promise,' said Emer. He doesn't want anyone to find out where his home is, she thought; he doesn't want Prince Brian raiding the settlement where his mother is. 'I won't tell anyone,' she said, and they rode on companionably together.

It was midday and the sun was high above their heads when they saw the first deer. It had just come through the trees into a clearing. They were downwind of it, so it didn't scent them. Instantly the men lifted their bows; five or six arrows flew through the air, and the deer fell dead in the clearing.

Conn lowered his bow hastily when he saw the deer fall. He hadn't even managed to get an arrow fitted to his bowstring in time, and he hoped no one had noticed. He glared aggressively at Ivar; but, to his relief, Ivar hadn't even got his bow completely off his back. He had been too busy talking to Emer.

Relief made Conn friendly. 'You and I will have to practise shooting,' he whispered to Ivar. 'When we go back, we'll set up a target inside the walls of the fort and we'll practise every day. We were both much too slow there.'

Ivar nodded. 'I haven't had much practice,' he confessed. 'At our settlement we were mostly just building boats for the warriors in Limerick. We didn't do much fighting.'

'Where was your settlement, Ivar?' asked Conn. Emer knew that Ivar wouldn't want to answer that question, and she wondered whether she should distract her brother, but she was too busy averting her eyes from the dead deer. It seemed so horrible to see it bounding through the forest one moment and lying dead on the ground the next. She could understand why Flann disliked the killing.

'How will you make your target?' she asked hurriedly, trying not to watch as Cormac and Patrick started to skin the deer.

Conn ignored her. 'Is your settlement near here, Ivar?' he went on, turning his back on his sister.

'Towards the south, I think,' said Ivar vaguely, glancing at the sky. 'It's by a river, a big river that goes down into the Shannon. When the boats are built, they're taken down the river and up towards Limerick.'

'The River Fergus?' asked a deep voice from behind them. 'I've a map that I've drawn here,' went on Prince Brian, pulling a tightly rolled scrap of skin from his pouch. 'Everywhere that I go in my brother's kingdom, I try to draw the place and fit it into what I already know. See, here's the river where your people's boats were, where the battle took place. That's the River Fergus.'

'But that's the name of our river,' cried Emer in surprise. 'At least, that's what we always call it. It rises in Lough Fergus.'

'It's probably the same, then,' said Prince Brian. 'Can you show me where it goes? Do you know, Conn? Where would your settlement be, Ivar?' he added, over his shoulder.

Emer and Conn got down from their ponies and puzzled over the little map which Prince Brian had smoothed out over his knee. Both of them were so absorbed in it that they didn't notice that Ivar hadn't answered Prince Brian's question.

'I think it must go along there,' said Conn, after a while. 'It does go underground for a bit. It goes down a deep cave. I went down ... I mean, I'm not allowed to go down there,' he went on hastily, with a quick glance around to make sure that his father wasn't listening.

'So it goes underground, does it?' said Brian, with

a half-smile. He's guessed that I went down there, thought Conn, but he won't say anything.

'Does it go underground for long?' Brian continued.

Conn shook his head. 'No, only for a few hundred paces; then it comes out again. After that it must go into Quin's Lake and then come out and go south, just past the place where we had the battle.'

'That must be right,' said Prince Brian, sounding satisfied. 'Now, Ivar,' he repeated, 'where is your settlement?'

Ivar looked at the map and shook his head dumbly.

'I should have said,' continued Brian gently, 'where is the settlement of the Vikings who stole your mother from her Irish home and kept her a prisoner among the enemies of her people?'

He's a clever man, thought Emer. It was obvious that Ivar didn't want to tell where his settlement was, didn't want to betray his own people. Clearly Brian hoped to persuade him by talk like this.

But Ivar was stubborn. Again he shook his head.

'I don't know,' he said, but once again his eyes wandered towards the south. He moved away from them and pretended to be very interested in the cutting up of the pieces of deer. Patrick and his two brothers were storing large chunks of meat in the saddle-bags which they had all brought. Even if no more deer were caught that day, this one alone would keep everyone in meat for a few weeks.

'I'm sure he does know,' said Conn. 'I'll get it out of him sometime, and then I'll tell you, Prince Brian. We can always rescue Ivar's mother, before killing everyone else.'

Emer said nothing, but she thought Ivar was right not to tell where his settlement was. She doubted whether the Irish warriors would be all that worried about rescuing Ivar's mother.

I know where the settlement is, though, she thought. She had seen Ivar's eyes rest on one part of the map, seen him flush slightly, seen how resolutely he had turned away from it. He knew how to get there, too. She guessed that. He had definitely recognised that clearing in the forest.

Later, when they were on their way again, she rode over to Ivar.

'Don't let Conn bully you into telling him anything you don't want to talk about,' she warned. 'He's quite nice, really, Conn is. But he's spoilt. Mother and Father think he's wonderful, and he's used to having his own way. He's very mean to Flann.'

'Flann is too much of a baby for a boy of his age,' said Ivar shortly. 'Conn is right.'

'Boys never have any sympathy for each other,' said Emer hotly. 'It's a good job that women and girls are so much nicer.'

She left him and went to join Brian Boru and her father, who were leading the party on through the dense forest of Kylemore. The two were talking earnestly, so she just rode quietly behind them.

'You see, Patrick,' Brian was saying, 'if I could mount some sort of raid — just a raid, with as little fighting as possible — on a Viking stronghold, and get back some of the treasure they've stolen from all the monasteries and abbeys of Ireland, then I would have enough to pay my men and to build up a good army. You can't have an army without food to put in their bellies, and weapons to put in their hands.'

Patrick said something that Emer couldn't hear, but Prince Brian's answering voice was as clear as ever.

'If needs be, we will; but the boy's settlement will be a small affair — just boat-builders and suchlike. Still, who knows — they may have some weapons that would be worth a raid.'

Emer drew back a little and glanced nervously around. Ivar was quite close to her. She wondered whether he had heard. It was hard to tell. Those pale-blue eyes of his gave very little away.

Chapter Six

The next morning, Conn and Ivar seemed to be the best of friends. Once the morning drills were finished and the boys' work of fetching water was over, the two of them began practising their archery, firing arrow after arrow into a bale of straw set up against one of the inner stone walls of the fort.

'That's no good,' said Emer scornfully, as she watched them. 'All you're doing is practising how far your shots can go. You need to make a proper target, with narrow circles in the middle, and just a dot in the very centre, and wide circles on the outside. I've seen one like that at the fair at Coad.'

'Well, you make one for us,' said Conn. 'That's girls' work, isn't it, Ivar?'

'Make it yourself,' snapped Emer. 'Unless....' An idea suddenly came to her, and she continued rapidly, 'Well, I will if you make me a bow and some arrows. You can do it while I'm making the target. You know how to do it; Father taught you. There are some nice young branches on that ash tree over there, beside the shrine of Saint Brigid. You can make a bow easily from one of them.'

'Oh, all right,' said Conn, 'but make sure that you make a good target.'

'I will,' replied Emer, and ran indoors to beg a piece of worn-out linen from Ita.

'You won't be able to use it for anything,' warned

Ita. 'It's so thin that you can see through it. What do you want it for?'

'It's for Conn,' muttered Emer, and her mother was satisfied. With his black curls and gentian-blue eyes and gorgeous smile, Conn could charm anything out of his mother.

By the time Emer came out again, Conn had cut a supple young branch from the ash tree and was showing Ivar how to bend it almost double and then whip a strip of rawhide around each end. Emer took a charred stick from her uncle Cormac's fire and, with a steady hand, drew an outer circle on the piece of linen; then she drew three more circles, each one inside the one before. In each circle she wrote a number. Then she made a small black circle, almost a dot, in the very centre. She took some of the rawhide and tied the target to the bale of straw. By the time Conn had made her bow, she was ready.

'I won't bother making you arrows today,' said Conn, his eyes lighting up at the sight of the target. 'You can borrow some of ours for today. What are the numbers for?'

'They're for scores,' said Emer smugly. 'We'll each have three goes and then we'll add up our marks. I'll help you if you get stuck,' she added kindly. Conn wasn't much good at adding up, although the monks at Kilfenora had done their best to teach him, just as they had taught her. 'You must let me go nearer the target than you, though. I'm much smaller and my muscles aren't so good.'

'All right,' said Conn, and then, impatiently, 'Oh, go away, Flann. You can't play with us.'

'Oh, let him,' said Emer. 'He can share my bow.'

'It's a girl's bow, anyway,' sneered Conn. 'It should

be just right for a girly-boy.'

'Stop being so mean,' said Emer, but it was no good. Flann burst into tears and ran away.

'You can have first shot,' said Conn hastily. 'Go on, you can go nearer than that. After all, it's your first time.'

Emer tried. Her arrow wavered through the air, touched the white cloth and fell to the ground.

'Have another go,' said Conn generously.

Very flushed, Emer fitted the arrow to the string, pulled back the bow with all her strength, and let the arrow fly. This time the arrow stuck in the bale, right through the outer circle.

'Oh, well done!' said Ivar.

'Great!' said Conn enthusiastically. No one can be nicer than Conn when he wants to be, thought Emer, running to pick up the two arrows.

'Well done,' said a deep voice behind them, and she turned around to see Prince Brian, Patrick and Cormac riding in through the eastern gate of the fort.

'I've got two sons and no daughter, my lord,' Patrick was saying with mock shame. Emer knew he was proud of her, though.

'No fear of that,' laughed Brian. 'With curls like that and eyes like that, there'll be plenty of young men along in no time, and then she'll turn back to a girl in the twinkling of an eye.'

Emer tossed her head. 'I don't see why a girl shouldn't learn to shoot. After all, if you all go off to war, we might get cattle-raiders here. I'm going to practise every day until I'm as good as Conn and Ivar.'

'What have you lot done to Flann?' demanded Deirdre, coming out of the little thatched house at the back of the fort and looking ready for any battle on behalf of her beloved boy.

'Why don't you let Flann play with you?' asked Patrick, as Flann appeared, tear-stained and red-eyed.

'I don't want to play shooting games,' said Flann sulkily.

'Well, what do you want to do?' shouted his father. 'I never see you do anything. You don't work, you don't play — you just mope around all day long!'

'I want to go back to the abbey!' shouted Flann, his face almost as red as his father's. 'I want to go on studying. I hate this place and I hate everyone in it!' He burst into loud sobs and ran back into the house, closely followed by his mother.

Emer and Conn looked at each other uneasily. They had never seen Flann like this before.

'Well — in that case....' Patrick shrugged his shoulders, avoiding looking at Cormac's face, which was purple with embarrassment and shame. Dismounting, he took Prince Brian's pony and his own and released them to crop the grass outside the walls. The weather was fine and dry, and Brian Boru's men were busy practising their swordplay, or helping with the digging of the vegetable gardens which lay in a circle outside the inner walls of the fort.

'We can stay here for a few months, Patrick,' Brian Boru said as they moved away. 'By then everyone's strength will have been built up, and with God's help we might be able to recruit some more men and take up the battle against the Vikings again.'

Conn beamed with delight. It was a great honour to have Prince Brian Boru, the King of Thomand's brother and heir, staying in their settlement. Perhaps by the time they marched against the Vikings again, he would be an important part of the army and no longer just a boy with his father.

With grim determination, he faced the target. 'We'll do two hours' practice, Ivar,' he said. 'No matter how sore our muscles are, we'll do two hours every single day.'

Emer wearied of the target practice long before they did, so she went out to play with the young ponies. These foals were her especial care, and she knew that Brian Boru wanted to buy them when they were fully grown. She had heard her father talk about it to her mother. Prince Brian and his men were sick of going long distances on foot. It all depended on him getting money or goods to pay for them, though, Ita had insisted. The ponies were their only way of feeding the family. The cattle all belonged to Cormac and Niall.

Emer was busy searching through the ponies' coats for any signs of ticks, which would suck their blood and make them unwell, when she saw Ivar and Conn — still good friends, apparently — going down towards the river. She remembered Conn's promise to Prince Brian that he would get Ivar to tell him where the Viking settlement was, and she wondered uneasily whether he had done it yet. Not yet, she thought. They've been shouting at the tops of their voices all the afternoon, and firing arrows and running to pick them up. Conn won't have had a chance to chat to Ivar; but he might be planning to do it now.

Both the boys had pieces of wood in their hands, and Emer remembered that Ivar had promised to teach Conn how to build a Viking boat.

'Wait for me,' she shouted. 'I'll come with you.'

Conn had won the shooting contest; she knew that

just by looking at him. His black curls were moist with sweat, his eyes were bluer than ever and his mouth was stretched in a delighted smile. Conn was always like that. He could never even play a game of chess for fun; he had to win, or he would be sulky for the rest of the day.

Ivar looked just the same, although the exercise had brought some pink to his cheeks. He obviously wasn't as worried about winning as Conn was. With his silver-blond hair and his pale-blue eyes, he was much handsomer than Conn, Emer thought — and then she grinned to herself, remembering how annoyed her mother had been when she had dared say that last night.

'Are you going to make a boat?' she asked as she joined them.

'Yes.' Ivar nodded. 'We go to the river to make a boat.'

His Irish was almost perfect, Emer thought, but occasionally the odd phrase sounded strange. She thought it made him even more fascinating.

'I'm going to make one, too,' said Conn. 'Then we're going to sail them on the River Fergus and see which one is the best.'

He sounded confident that his would be the best. He couldn't imagine that the Viking boy could possibly beat him at anything.

'I'll run back and cut off two pieces of the linen that I used for the target,' said Emer. 'You can use them for sails. You remember, Conn, you told me that the boats each had a big square sail in the centre.'

Emer ran back and, with her knife, cut the two pieces of linen. Then she ran into the little Cathaireen Field, just next to the fort, and picked a few sloes.

She cut them in half and squeezed the purple juice down the centre of each sail, in two stripes. Now the sails looked just as Conn had described them.

By the time Emer reached the river meadows, she could see that Conn was getting bored with Ivar's instructions.

'It's not worth the trouble, cutting all those planks — oh, all right, *strakes*, then,' he added, as Ivar opened his mouth to correct him. 'Why can't we make the sides out of two pieces instead of ten? It's just a waste of time.'

Ivar shrugged. 'You do it your way, then. I'm just trying to show you how I've been taught.'

'Show me how to do it, Ivar,' said Emer. She watched carefully as he worked slowly and steadily, shaving the wood off the tiny strakes and fastening the crossbeams to the hull.

'You see,' he said, 'the sharper the prow — that's the top bit of the boat — the quicker it goes through the water. And look at that bit at the bottom of the boat — that's called the keel. I'll shave the keel, too, so that it also goes easily through the water.'

Out of the corner of her eye, Emer could see that Conn was listening. Quickly he picked up his uncle Niall's spokeshave and tried to fine down his rather clumsy-looking prow. Even at this stage, his boat didn't look as good as Ivar's.

There wasn't much conversation for the next half-hour. Ivar worked away, happily humming to himself, occasionally stopping his busy shaving and shaping to explain something to Emer. Conn kept taking his boat down to the water's edge and then coming back, frowning and glancing surreptitiously at Ivar's neat and elegant boat and making hasty changes to his own.

At the end of the half-hour, he lost patience.

'Oh, come on,' he said roughly. 'It'll be supper-time soon. If we don't do it now, we'll never do it.'

'Another few minutes,' said Ivar, without raising his head from his boat. He was stuffing the minute spaces between the strakes with tiny pieces of moss.

'You understand, if we were making this the right way and taking proper time over it, these cracks would be stuffed with moss and then tar would be painted over them, to keep the moss in place and stop the water getting into the boat,' he explained.

Conn smiled — not one of his nice smiles, Emer noticed. This was more like the smile that he had when he was going to checkmate her at the end of a game of chess.

'I understand,' he said airily. 'If your boat sinks, then it will be because you haven't had enough time to make it the right way.'

Ivar said nothing, though the colour rose in his cheeks.

Flann had come creeping down through a gap in the wall that surrounded the fort. Emer tried to make herself smile at him. She didn't like Flann that much; he was a ridiculous baby for his age. However, that was probably more his mother's fault than his own. Ita had once told Emer privately that Deirdre and Cormac had lost five sons, one after the other, before Flann had been born. That was probably why Deirdre always tried to protect him from everything.

Emer looked at Flann sympathetically and patted the grass beside her. 'Come and watch, Flann,' she said.

'Now for the mast,' said Ivar, fitting the little twig carefully into the hole he had prepared. 'Give me the sail, Emer.'

Conn had forgotten about the sail, and they had to wait while he hastily hacked out a hole. He stuck in his mast and tied on the sail. Ivar opened his mouth to say something and then shut it firmly. Emer half-smiled to herself. Even to her, Conn's mast looked too tall and too heavy.

'We'll both wade into the centre of the river,' ordered Conn. 'It's only about three feet deep here. Emer, you count to three, and Flann, you run up and stand by the bridge and catch the boats as they come up. The first one to reach Flann is the winner. Go on, Flann, hurry up.'

'I'm not allowed to get wet,' objected Flann.

Conn gave a heavy sigh. 'Are you allowed to count up to three?' he asked sarcastically.

Flann looked uncertain. 'Yes,' he replied, after a pause.

Emer ran down the bank and waded out until she was right in the centre near the bridge. The water was cold, but it didn't bother her. She knew which boat would win. She was certain of it.

She wasn't quite prepared for what happened, though. Ivar's boat sped along like a bird, skimming the top of the flow, while Conn's hardly moved. At last a ripple of water caught it; but, instead of moving forward, it spun around and around. Then the heavy mast toppled it and it sank like a stone. Instinctively, Emer reached out and caught Ivar's boat, while Ivar doubled up with laughter and even Flann gave a few feeble chuckles.

'Shut up, shut up!' yelled Conn, lashing out with his fists. 'Shut up, you Viking bastard. Don't you laugh at me or I'll kill you!'

'I'm not a bastard!' cried Ivar through gritted

teeth, doing his best to land a few punches on Conn's barrel-like chest. 'Anyway, I'm not laughing at you. I'm laughing at your stupid boat. You wouldn't listen to me and you wouldn't learn from me, so you made a stupid boat.'

Conn gave a howl of rage. Emer moved upstream to try to separate them. Flann bolted back up the hill like a frightened rabbit.

Then Conn stopped, deliberately turned his back on Ivar and waded out of the stream.

'Well, anyway,' he said over his shoulder, 'you may not be a bastard, but you'll soon be an orphan. Brian Boru is going to raid your settlement, and your father and mother will be killed.'

Chapter Seven

Emer woke with a start. Someone had a hand over her mouth.

The fire flamed up at that moment, filling the little house with a glow of light. She sighed with relief: it was only Conn. What was he doing there, though? Ever since Brian Boru and his men had arrived, Conn had slept down in the underground room with the other soldiers.

She struggled, and he took his hand away and signed to her to follow him outside. She pulled her bratt on over her tunic and followed him out. The blackness of the night had faded to a sort of grey, and the eastern sky was pale gold at the horizon.

'What's the matter?' hissed Emer. 'What are you waking me up at this time for?'

'It's Ivar,' whispered Conn. 'He crept out of the underground room a little while ago. When I got out, he was gone. One of the ponies is gone, too. He's taken Primrose and she's the fastest of all the ponies.'

'But what's the matter?' said Emer, still half-asleep. 'He's probably gone for a ride. You know today is a holiday. You told me yourself. Prince Brian said that everyone had a holiday from drilling today.'

Conn shook his head. 'You're forgetting about the fight we had, and ... and what I said to him,' he said, looking embarrassed and ashamed.

'What? About him being a bastard?'

'No — I didn't really mean that. No, I mean about Prince Brian raiding his settlement and killing his father and his mother.'

Emer was silent. She remembered now. She remembered the look on Ivar's face, and how he had refused to eat any supper and had gone off by himself and spoken to no one.

'I think he's gone back to his settlement to warn them,' Conn went on.

'I might never see him again,' said Emer sadly.

'No — you don't understand! Can't you see how dangerous it is? I've put the whole of Drumshee in danger with my stupid temper. I think he'll bring a party of Vikings here. He knows the way now. If he can find the way to his settlement, he can find the way back here. And it's all my fault. I wish I'd never said that. Actually, I wished I hadn't said it the moment after I spoke.'

Emer was startled, less by what he said than by the fact that Conn would acknowledge that he had done something stupid or wrong. She began to think hard. Would Ivar really bring a party of Vikings to raid Drumshee and kill Brian Boru and his soldiers? She had always felt that he hated his father and the other Vikings. If he had gone back, it was for his mother's sake.

'I'd better go and tell Prince Brian,' said Conn despairingly. His face had gone very white, Emer saw. He almost looked as if he would burst into tears.

'No, wait,' she said. 'Wait, let me think.'

'The trouble is that I don't know which way he's gone,' Conn went on, not taking any notice of her. 'If only I knew, I could go after him.'

'Yes, but I do, I think,' said Emer rapidly. 'I'm sure

I could lead you there, but you'll have to promise me something first.'

'I'll promise anything,' said Conn solemnly.

'Promise that you'll never, ever tell Prince Brian, or anyone else, where Ivar's settlement is. If you don't promise, then I won't show you the way.'

'I promise,' said Conn.

'By the Virgin Mary and all the angels and saints?'

'By the Virgin Mary and all the angels and saints,' repeated Conn. 'But how are we going to explain where Ivar went?'

'We won't. We'll say we all went fishing,' said Emer. 'You go and get two ponies, and I'll tell Mother.'

The little house was still in darkness when she returned, but she went to the curtained-off enclosure where her parents slept and knelt on the floor beside her sleeping mother.

'Conn and Ivar and I are going fishing,' she whispered. 'Don't worry about us. It might be late when we come back.'

Ita murmured sleepily, but Emer didn't wait for any questions or objections. Quickly she picked up a couple of loaves from beside the central fireplace. Her mother had baked them on the iron plate the night before, and they were still warm and crusty. She put a piece in her mouth and went out to join Conn.

'Here you are,' she said, breaking off another piece of bread and handing it to him. She put the rest in her pouch and vaulted onto her pony. Conn had his bow and arrows on his back, she noticed, and his sword in his belt.

'Conn,' she said, while he still had his mouth full, 'you'll have to promise me something else. If Ivar wants to rescue his mother, then we'll help him and bring her back to Drumshee. Do you promise?'

Conn nodded, then swallowed the piece of bread and said, 'I promise.' He sounded rather reluctant, Emer thought. He didn't like that idea, probably because then he would have to explain everything to his hero, Prince Brian. She was satisfied that he would keep his promise, though. That was one of the good things about Conn: he always kept his word. She kicked her heels lightly, shook the pony's reins and turned him to the left, going down the lane towards the Isle of Maain and the great forest of Kylemore beyond.

'How do you know where to go, anyway?' asked Conn.

'Just follow me,' said Emer firmly. She had no intention of telling Conn about the tree blasted by lightning or any other landmark. In fact, when they reached the tree, after an hour of hard riding, she herself wasn't sure where to go next. She remembered Prince Brian's map, though, with the forest of Kylemore marked on it, and, to the east, the curving path of the great River Fergus — three times as wide there as it was at Drumshee — leading into the River Shannon and then joining the sea.

'Conn,' she said, 'do you remember what Ivar said about building the boats? Where did they build them? Was it in their settlement?'

'It was beside the river,' said Conn, a faint trace of embarrassment in his face as he recalled the afternoon before. 'But the river was just next to the settlement. Ivar told me they built the boat next to the river so that it would be easy to launch it.'

And they carried the trees from Kylemore Forest,

thought Emer; so it must be to the east of here. It won't be too far, either. They couldn't have dragged a huge oak tree too many miles through the forest. Now that she looked about her carefully, she could see the marks where they had dragged the tree. There were deep ruts which had filled up with brown and yellow leaves.

'What's the matter?' asked Conn anxiously. 'Don't you know where to go?'

'Follow me,' repeated Emer confidently, urging her pony to a slow trot and keeping her eye on the leaf-filled ruts.

They rode for another half-hour, and then Conn gave a cry of triumph.

'Look at that, Emer!' He held out a long, waving wand of bramble. 'Look — that's some hair from Primrose's mane. I'd know that colour anywhere.'

Emer nodded. He was right: it was definitely Primrose's mane. A warm feeling of relief swept over her. They would find Ivar, after all.

She pulled up her pony and held up her hand. 'Wait,' she said. 'Listen. Do you hear something?'

Conn pulled up his pony, and the forest became very quiet. Emer listened intently. She had been right. It was a sound that they only heard from their own River Fergus when it was in full flood, but it was, without any doubt at all, the sound of a river.

'It's the river,' said Conn. 'Is that where the settlement is?'

'Let's follow the path,' Emer said, ignoring his question. 'Keep looking for any more of Primrose's hair. Her coat is quite long now, with the winter coming on.'

They saw two more pieces of Primrose's mane

before the forest began to thin out and the light began to come strongly through the trees.

'Do you notice that all the trees here are quite small?' said Conn, in an undertone. 'You can see all the stumps of the big trees that they've cut down.'

At that moment, Emer gave an exclamation. 'Look!' she said, and pointed.

They had just come around a thick clump of osier willows, and suddenly they were almost on top of the Viking settlement. There, by the side of the river, were ten or twelve long, low houses, their walls made from woven twigs of osier and alder, their roofs thatched with reeds from the river.

'Shhh,' said Conn softly.

He got off his pony and led him behind the clump of osiers. Emer followed him, and they carefully parted the soft twigs of the osiers and peered out. Now they could see, but not be seen.

By the side of the river was the outline of a huge ship. Only the hull had been made so far, and it was kept upright by logs set in the ground. Eight or nine men were fastening crossbeams inside the hull, from side to side, and a tall man with silver-blond hair and a jaw the shape of a lantern was standing by the side of the boat, bellowing orders. Suddenly Emer felt quite sure that the tall man was Ivar's father. He looked very bad-tempered, and Emer felt sorry for Ivar.

She looked all around carefully, but there was no sign of Ivar himself. Over at the settlement there were several women, some of them talking, some dipping buckets in the stream which ran beside the houses, others playing with children, and two of them dipping huge pieces of canvas into a bath full of some red liquid and then hanging the dripping cloths on wooden frames. They must be making sails for the ships, thought Emer. Ivar had told her that the Vikings liked their sails to be blood-red, as they thought that this frightened their enemies.

'Look,' whispered Conn. 'Look at that house in the corner, over there — the one farthest from the river, behind the red cloths.'

Emer looked. There was something silver moving there, quite near to the ground. At first she thought it was a silver-haired small child, but then she realised that it was Ivar; he was bent double, moving slowly and carefully, keeping behind the shelter of the huge cloths.

From behind Conn and Emer came the sudden whinny of a pony. Their own ponies whinnied in response.

Ivar threw a hunted glance over his shoulder and obviously decided to run. He shot across the grass with the speed of an arrow, his long legs covering the ground more quickly than Emer would have imagined possible. As he came nearer, she could see that Ivar's face was smeared with tears and that he was sobbing. He passed them without even seeming to see them.

'Quick,' said Conn, from beside her. 'Quick, get on your pony. Be ready to follow him. That's Primrose over there; I know her voice. Listen, she's greeting him.'

Ivar clearly hadn't seen them. As they followed him, Emer could hear his sobbing above the sound of Primrose's feet.

'What's happened to him, Conn?' she whispered urgently.

'I don't know,' said Conn impatiently. 'We must catch him. That's not the way back to Drumshee; he's going in the opposite direction.' He kicked his heels against the pony's sides and tore after Ivar.

Emer followed, keeping pace with him. The trouble was that Ivar was a really good rider. If he kept going like that, they would never be able to pass him.

She gave a quick look over her shoulder. They were going so fast that the Viking settlement had disappeared from their sight, and they could no longer hear the shouts of the men and the shrill voices of the children. She decided to risk it.

'Ivar!' she shouted. 'Stop! It's me, Emer.'

It was the last thing Ivar had expected. He pulled on the reins so quickly that Primrose reared up on her hind legs and Ivar almost fell off. Quickly he recovered himself and got the pony under control. Then, reluctantly, he turned to face Emer and Conn.

They both looked at him, not knowing what to say. Conn, especially, was embarrassed and awkward. He nudged Emer, but Emer couldn't think of anything to say either.

At last, in desperation, Conn muttered, 'It's a nice day, isn't it?'

This sounded so stupid that Emer began to laugh. Then Conn did as well, and finally Ivar laughed, a little hysterically, and scrubbed his eyes with the end of his bratt.

'Come on,' said Conn. 'You're going the wrong way. Let's go home.'

They rode for about ten minutes without speaking. Something will have to be said, thought Emer. Ivar looked much better; he had definitely stopped crying, and he was beginning to get some colour back in his cheeks.

'Let's stop here,' she said. 'I'm starving. I've got

enough bread for all of us.'

They all sat on the ivy-covered trunk of a fallen tree and bit into the crusty bread. Emer nudged Conn hard; when he didn't take the hint, she said sharply, 'Haven't you got something to say, Conn?'

'I'm sorry I lost my temper,' mumbled Conn.

Ivar said nothing, but his colour rose. He picked up a twig and busied himself poking it into an ants' nest.

Conn looked at Emer in desperation, but she refused to look at him. This is something he has to do by himself, she thought firmly.

'I didn't really mean what I said,' Conn went on. 'Prince Brian doesn't know where your settlement is, and I've promised Emer that I'll never tell anyone. I've sworn by the Virgin Mary and all the angels and saints,' he added, though he wasn't sure that Ivar would know what he meant. The Vikings were pagans, and they believed in strange gods like Thor, the god of thunder, and Odin, the god of war.

Ivar seemed to understand what Conn meant, however, because he nodded. He didn't say anything, though, and Conn couldn't think of anything else to say. He munched another mouthful of bread and looked at Emer appealingly.

She took pity on him. At least he had apologised, which wasn't something he ever liked to do. It was up to her to find out what had happened.

'What about your mother, Ivar?' she asked gently. 'Did you see her?'

To her and Conn's horror, Ivar's eyes filled with tears again. He leant over and poked at the ants' nest, bending down so that his face couldn't be seen.

'I saw her,' he said, in a choked voice. 'I asked her

to come away with me. We could live in the forest. I could build her a house. I would be able to shoot hares and gather wild fruit. We could have lived there.'

He stopped.

'What did she say?' prompted Emer.

'She said no. She told me to go away. She said I made trouble. She said she was better off without me....' He swallowed another sob. 'She said that I'm old enough to look after myself, and that things have been much better between her and my father since I went away. He told her that I ran away and joined the Irish. She said I should go back to the Irish and not come to see her again.' After a moment, Ivar added in a low voice, 'I think she's expecting another baby. Anyway, she doesn't want me.'

There was an awkward silence. Then Emer rose to her feet, shaking the crumbs from her bratt and her tunic.

'Let's go,' she said. She couldn't think of anything else to say. How awful to have a mother who didn't want you! she thought.

'Yes, let's go,' said Conn with relief. 'When we get back we'll have a great time. We'll go fishing, and practise our archery, and ... and will you show me how to make another boat? I didn't really listen to you the last time, but I'd like to make one just like the one you made. It was brilliant.'

Ivar couldn't speak, but he punched Conn on the arm, and Conn punched him back, just to show that there were no hard feelings. They all jumped onto their ponies and set off for Drumshee.

Chapter Eight

The ride back was easy and pleasant. Conn was at his most charming. He was relieved that everything had worked out so well; and, to give him his due, thought Emer, he was genuinely shocked at Ivar's mother not wanting him to come back. Of course, Ita thought Conn was the most wonderful boy in the world, so it would seem especially strange to him that Ivar's mother felt so differently about her son. In fact, thought Emer, we're both pretty lucky in our parents. Even if Conn was his mother's especial darling, she was her father's, and they both knew that Patrick and Ita loved their two children.

She looked at Ivar and tried to think of something nice to say to him.

'I think you're very handsome, Ivar,' she said in a motherly tone. 'I wish I had hair the colour of yours.'

Ivar was a bit taken aback. 'Oh, thanks,' he said. 'You are, too,' he added, glancing quickly at Conn to see if he was laughing at him.

Conn did laugh, but only in a nice way — not at all the way he sneered at poor Flann. Emer felt very proud of her brother. He's pretty handsome himself, she thought; but she had no intention of telling him. If he just went on being so nice, Ivar might start to feel better.

All the way back to Drumshee, Conn asked Ivar questions about boats and boat-building and listened carefully to what he had to say. It was only when they were passing the bog where they cut their turf for the fire that he suddenly remembered what they were supposed to be doing. He pulled up his pony.

'Oh, bother,' he said. 'We forgot. We're supposed to be fishing. What'll they say if we arrive with no fish?'

'Oh, we'll just say that there were no fish around today,' said Emer impatiently. She was sure that her mother wouldn't care. There was plenty of deer meat around and it wasn't a very good time for fishing.

'We'd better get back,' she added. 'It'll be sundown soon. What are you looking at, Ivar?'

Ivar had his eyes screwed up against the glare of the sunbeams from the west. 'There seem to be a lot of men over there. Listen — you can hear the sound of ponies on the road. Where are they all going? Is it Prince Brian?'

'It's definitely Prince Brian and the rest of the men,' said Conn, shielding his eyes with his hand. 'Where are they going?'

'Let's go home and find out,' said Emer, yawning slightly. She had been up early and had ridden all day. Now she felt ready for a nice supper and a doze by the fire.

'Maybe they go to hunt?' suggested Ivar.

'No,' said Conn impatiently. 'They're going in the wrong direction. They're going towards Kilfenora, towards the abbey. Maybe there's trouble there. You go home, Emer, and we'll follow them.'

With that he was gone, thundering down the lane beside the Rough Field, going so fast that it looked as if he would overtake the men in a few minutes. Without a glance at Emer, Ivar followed behind.

'Wait!' shouted Emer. 'I'm coming with you.'

They didn't show any signs of hearing, but she followed them all the same, her tiredness forgotten. Why would Prince Brian and his men gallop at such a rate towards Kilfenora, unless there was some danger to the abbey?

At the thought of the gentle monks there who had taught her, and tried to teach Conn, Emer was filled with anger. She urged her pony on. Even so, Conn and Ivar were at the outskirts of Kilfenora by the time she caught up with them.

'Go back!' said Conn furiously. 'Can't you see what's happening? There's a battle going on!' He pulled his sword from his belt and charged down the hill, to the curving street which flanked the abbey and the monks' cottages.

'Go back,' repeated Ivar, pulling out his sword. He hesitated, looking back at Emer.

'Remember that you're not armed,' he said gently. 'I know the Vikings. They do terrible things to women.'

'Well, one of them might go after me if I start to ride home, then. I'd better stay. Then I can shout if I need help.'

He looked dubious, but nodded. 'I suppose you're right. Look, stay hidden behind that clump of black-thorn over there.'

Emer nodded. 'All right,' she said. Ivar gave a satisfied nod and galloped after Conn.

Emer stayed where she was. She had no intention of going home, but Ivar was probably right: it would be silly to go down into Kilfenora. She was quite safe on the hillside. She could see everything that was going on, and she could easily escape if any Vikings came towards her.

So these were the Vikings — tall, many of them

silver-haired like Ivar, some wearing coats of mail and steel helmets. Their bloodcurdling cries filled the air and they fought with great ferocity.

Emer caught sight of her father. He was beside Brian Boru, at his left side, his long sword clashing against any Viking axe that came near his prince. She could see Conn and Ivar, their swords flashing, struggling to make their way down the street. She held her breath. Time after time, it seemed as if one or the other must fall to a Viking axe; but each time the agile boys ducked and twisted and managed to escape. They reached Patrick, and Emer began to breathe more easily.

To the west of the abbey she saw a large cart, drawn by four horses. It was piled high with gold and silver cups, precious books bound in vellum, and altar cloths with gold embroidery. The Vikings had obviously loaded it before Prince Brian and his men arrived. They couldn't have got all that from Kilfenora, Emer thought. They must have gone to another abbey or two, on their way up from Limerick.

The Irish seemed to be getting the better of them, though. The Vikings hadn't expected any resistance, except from a few farmers with billhooks and spades, and they had been met by disciplined and well-trained troops. Little by little, they were being driven into the market square, with Brian Boru's troops surrounding them like a pack of hungry wolves around a cluster of fat sheep.

At that moment, an unexpected sound cut through the cries and shrieks and curses. It was the sound of the abbey bell, which rang out across the stony land-scape every four hours. But this wasn't the ordinary solemn clanging; this was a wild, jangled explosion of sound. All other noise died down, and everyone looked up towards the tower.

Then the Vikings gave a great shout of triumph. At the top of the tower, with the bell-rope tied around his neck, was the tall figure of Abbot Finguirt, abbot of Kilfenora.

Emer froze. Were the Vikings really going to hang that gentle old man who had taught her and Conn and Flann so patiently? She stared at the tower, horrified.

'Stand still, all you Irish — no one move!' shouted the Viking leader. He was standing on the tower, behind the abbot, holding the rope in his hand. 'If anyone follows the cart, this man will die.'

Emer, looking down, saw Brian Boru reluctantly lower his sword arm. Her father did the same. Beside him, just coming up to his shoulder, were the two boys. She could see the black head and the silver head; as she looked, she saw the silver head move close to the black one, so close that they might have been embracing, or whispering. Then, slowly and casually, the silver head moved away and mingled with the other silver heads of the victorious Vikings.

The great cart, laden with spoil from the abbeys, trundled down the road, going to the east. Most of the Vikings jumped onto their horses and followed it, leaving their leader in the tower and a group of men waiting in the street in front of the church, to make sure that no Irishman reached for his sword until their leader was safely down and mounted on his horse.

Conn had moved a little away from his father and Brian Boru. Emer strained her eyes to see what he was doing, and gasped. Quietly, just by letting one shoulder sag, he had shrugged his bow off his back, and he was fitting an arrow to the string. Surely he couldn't be stupid enough to think that he could shoot the Viking leader from that distance? He would be killed the instant that he let fly. No one was looking at him for the moment, but that was because he was only a boy. Emer stared at him in an agony of fear.

The next minute, everything changed. Suddenly a silver head appeared on the tower, a knife flashed, the rope was severed, Abbot Finguirt was dragged backwards, the bell jangled and a clear boyish voice rang out from the street:

'Don't move, you Vikings — don't move! I have your leader covered, and I'm the best archer in Brian Boru's army.'

Trust Conn to boast! Emer was laughing and crying at the same time. She could see her father's expression, but Brian Boru hadn't moved a muscle. The Vikings were obviously stunned and unsure how much to believe. They hesitated, and then they were lost. The abbot disappeared from the tower; then Ivar's silver head was gone as well, and instantly Brian Boru gave the signal to attack. A shower of arrows, Conn's among them, winged their way to the tower; the Viking leader fell dead, and a great shout rose up from the Irish.

'Brian *abú!*' they yelled, and then they swept into the attack.

It was too late to save the treasure, but the monks were all safe. The fighting didn't last long. One by one the Vikings were cut down, and by the time Emer made her way down to the village street, the battle was over.

Patrick had an arm around each of the boys.

'Well done, you two,' Prince Brian was saying.

'Today you saved us all. I'll never forget that. If I ever become King of Thomand, you two will be captains in my army.'

'It was Ivar's idea,' said Conn honestly. 'He whispered it to me. He thought the Vikings wouldn't notice him moving around, because of his silver hair. They would just think he was one of their boys. Go on, Ivar, tell them.'

'Well, I crept around to the back of the tower, and when no one was looking, I went up the stairs and just cut the rope off the abbot's neck and pulled him back. I rang the bell once. That was the signal to Conn, and he shouted out.'

'I just said that about being the best archer in order to frighten them,' said Conn hastily, as he saw a smile touch Prince Brian's lips at the memory of his words. 'I know I'm not much good, really, but Ivar and I are going to practise every day until we become good.'

'Whatever was the truth of it, it worked,' said Brian Boru dryly. 'Two soldiers who can think as quickly as you two are always going to be valuable to me.'

Emer glowed with pride in them both. She wished that she had been armed and could have joined the battle too. Still, perhaps it was just as well that she hadn't. Already her father was beginning to fuss about her being there at all. If Patrick hadn't been bursting with pride about Conn, he would have been demanding to know why he had brought his sister into danger.

'Here's the abbot, come to thank his deliverers,' said Brian Boru.

Abbot Finguirt's thanks were long and profuse, with many offers of perpetual prayers for the two boys. Ivar listened politely, but Conn was visibly bored. He wanted to hear more praise from Brian Boru. In another minute he'll walk off, thought Emer. I'll have to distract Father Abbot's attention from him.

'Did you lose much treasure, Father?' she asked hastily.

The abbot turned to her. 'I fear so, Emer,' he said sadly. 'We've lost our sacred cups and our altar cloths — but, worst of all, we've lost our most precious book, the Psalter of King David. I fear these pagans have taken it back to Limerick with them.'

He turned to Brian Boru. 'Is there any hope that you might be able to get it back for us, my son?'

Brian Boru shook his head regretfully. 'Not today, Father. We are still greatly outnumbered. There would be no point in pursuing them; they'll probably meet up with others quite near here. But one thing I can promise you, Father: I will never rest until I can make a raid on Limerick. With young men like these two growing up, who knows what we'll be able to do in the future?'

This brought the attention back to Conn again, and a beaming smile crossed his lips, making him look more like an angel than a boy.

'Can we go home now?' he asked. 'I want supper. All this fighting has made me ever so hungry.'

~

That night, Brian Boru didn't go back to the underground room after the evening meal; he stayed in the little round house, talking to Patrick beside the fire. Emer and her mother went to bed, but the two men sat on by the fire. From behind the skins which curtained off her bed of animal skins piled on straw, Emer could hear the rise and fall of their voices.

'I've thought and thought,' Brian Boru was saying. 'I know I must have money to build up an army. The only place I can get money is from the Vikings' hoard of looted treasure at Limerick, and I can't attack Limerick unless I have a good army at my back. My mind keeps going around in that circle.'

'What about a quick raid?' suggested Patrick. 'In and out again, with as little fighting as possible.'

'No,' said Brian, and Emer could hear the regret in his voice. 'No, Limerick is too well guarded. It has the Shannon all around. We'd never get past the guards. No, it's a battle or nothing. But I can't fight a battle without troops, and I can't get troops — except a handful of dedicated men — without having the means to feed them, clothe them and pay them. No, there's no help for it: if I can't get my hands on some gold or silver soon, I'll have to return to my brother's court and do as he does — speak false soft words to the Vikings and allow them to go on robbing and pillaging Ireland.'

Emer strained her ears to hear what her father said in reply, but Patrick had no words of comfort to give his beloved prince. Soon she heard them part at the door of the little house. Her eyes were wet with tears. It had been such an exciting day, and it had seemed to end so well; and now to hear this tone of despair from the leader....

To distract herself, she began to think about Ivar. It was lovely that he had come back to Drumshee with them, and it was even lovelier that he and Conn seemed to have become such good friends. They had sat side by side during supper, each with an arm around the other's shoulders, planning the boats they would make and how they would test them....

Suddenly Emer sat bolt upright on her bed. *Boats!* she thought. That's it! That's the way to do it!

She was so excited that she almost got out of bed and went down to the underground room to tell Conn and Ivar all about it, but then she laughed at herself. Tomorrow would be soon enough. They would talk it over, all three of them, and then they would go and see Prince Brian. If he approved of the idea, the work could be started immediately.

Chapter Nine

Breakfast had never seemed so long to Emer as it did the following day. The men were all lively and pleased with themselves after their victory over the Vikings. They were hungry, as well, and plate after plate of porridge was eaten. Emer saw her mother give a worried glance at the big pot full of oats. That was the family's store for the winter, and if the men went on eating like this, it would be used up by Christmas.

Prince Brian noticed Ita's look; his face grew darker and he became more silent. Emer longed for breakfast to be over so she could tell Conn and Ivar her plan. Then they could all three go to Prince Brian, and perhaps the look of despair would vanish from his face.

'You should have been there, Flann,' Conn was saying to his cousin. 'You would have loved it. All that blood everywhere.'

'Oh, leave him alone, Conn, he's only a child,' came Ivar's voice, and for once Conn didn't start fighting with Ivar instead. He knows that Ivar did the most dangerous thing yesterday, thought Emer. Now he respects Ivar and he listens to him.

'Never mind, Flann,' she whispered, as her cousin came towards the fire, wiping the marks of tears from his cheeks. 'Conn's only teasing. He's always trying to tease me, too, but I never take any notice of him, so he soon stops.'

Someone should stop him, though, she thought. Father should stop him, or Uncle Cormac. Flann's just getting worse and worse. It's not good for him. He spends most of his time in tears whenever he's away from his mother. He'll never grow up to be a man if he goes on like this.

'Conn,' she called out, as he was moving away from the table. 'Come here for a minute. I want to talk to you.'

'You sound like Mother when she's in a temper,' teased Conn, coming up and giving one of her curls a tug.

'Stop it!' Emer said, slapping his face as hard as she could. She knew Conn wouldn't dare hit her back; their father wasn't far away. From the corner of her eye she could see Flann looking at her in shock and horror.

'Now look, Conn,' she said, feeling pleased with herself, 'I want you to make me a promise. I want you to promise not to tease Flann for a week. Just give him seven days of peace. You must promise me now, and you must promise God when we go to mass in Kilfenora this morning.'

'Oh, must I?' said Conn scornfully. 'Do you hear her, Ivar? Who's going to make me?'

'I am,' said Emer firmly. She lowered her voice so that Flann couldn't hear and moved a little closer to Conn and Ivar.

'Prince Brian is thinking of going back to his brother,' she whispered. 'I heard him talking to Father last night. The only way he can stay here at Drumshee and train his army is if he gets hold of some Viking treasure — the silver and gold they stole from Irish churches and monasteries and abbeys.'

She stopped and looked at both boys. She had to make them believe in her idea, but first she had to get Conn to promise.

'I suddenly got the most wonderful idea last night,' she went on, 'but I'm not telling you until you promise.'

'Oh, I promise,' said Conn impatiently. 'I'm tired of hearing the little runt snivel, anyway. Go on, Ivar — you promise, too. You were teasing him last night, as well.'

'I promise,' said Ivar, looking a little embarrassed and avoiding Emer's eyes.

'Don't worry,' said Emer, looking at him kindly. 'I've teased Flann myself, I have to admit, but I think we should stop. It's not making him better; it's making him worse.'

'What's your plan, Emer?' asked Ivar. He looked at her and smiled, and suddenly everything seemed possible.

'Could you build a boat, Ivar?' she asked. 'A full-sized boat, I mean; not a toy one.'

He nodded. 'Yes, but I wouldn't be able to do it all by myself. I'm not strong enough. I would need help.'

'You'll have plenty,' Emer told him. She felt like a princess at that moment. 'I can give you twenty men.'

'What on earth are you talking about?' demanded Conn.

'Oh, Conn,' Emer said wearily. 'It's no wonder the brothers in Kilfenora couldn't teach you anything. Can't you see what I'm getting at?'

Ivar was nodding. 'It is clever. I remember the map that Brian Boru has. Yes, we could do it.'

Conn's colour rose. For a moment he almost looked like Flann when they teased him. 'What are you talking about?' he shouted.

Emer saw her father look over. She grabbed Conn by the arm and pulled him aside, into the corner near the fire. It would be a pity if he lost his temper and refused to have anything to do with talking to Brian Boru.

'I'm just going to tell you, Conn,' she said. 'My idea is that Ivar should teach everyone here, not just you, how to build a boat — a real boat. Then, when it's built, Prince Brian and his men can sail down the River Fergus and back up that other big river....'

'The Shannon,' put in Ivar.

'The Vikings at Limerick won't expect anyone to arrive by river. Prince Brian said that Limerick is completely surrounded by the River Shannon, except for the very south of it, didn't he? So all the guards will be on that south side and on the bridges. So if Prince Brian's men go by boat, by the river, from the north-west, they might be able to raid Limerick and carry away enough goods — gold, silver, anything else — to let Prince Brian build up his army here at Drumshee.'

Conn was silent, biting his lip, his eyes fixed on the ground. He wished he had thought of it himself, Emer knew, but she wasn't going to say any more. He had to decide for himself which was the most important: his pride, or Prince Brian.

When he looked up, she knew that the nice side of him had won. His dark-blue eyes were blazing with excitement. He pulled her curls again, but she knew it was only in fun.

'Come on!' he said. 'What are we waiting for?

Let's go and see Prince Brian.'

Brian was standing moodily by himself, watching his men, who were washing themselves, trimming their moustaches, combing their hair and getting themselves as clean and tidy as possible for the midday mass at Kilfenora church.

'My lord,' said Conn, his boy's voice breaking a little with excitement, 'my sister has an idea, and I think it's a good one. Would you let her explain?'

Brian roused himself and gave Emer his usual warm smile. 'What is it?' he asked. 'I could do with a few ideas now.'

Emer faced him boldly. This was not the time to be shy.

'Ivar's father is a boat-builder,' she said, and she saw a spark of interest come into Brian's eyes. 'He taught Ivar to build boats. If your men helped him, Ivar could build a boat that would take you to Limerick. I heard you talking to Father last night. If you went by the River Shannon, in a Viking boat, you could surprise the Vikings at Limerick, and you might be able to take back some of the treasure they stole.'

Brian looked at her silently for a moment and then shocked her by suddenly starting to laugh.

Emer felt embarrassed, and then annoyed. 'It's a good plan,' she insisted.

Brian recovered himself. 'It's a great plan, my dear,' he said. 'I'm only laughing to think that I might be saved by a little girl and two lads.'

He turned to Ivar. 'Would you do this for us, Ivar?' he asked. 'Would you help us?'

'Yes, my lord,' said Ivar. 'As long as there will be no attack on the settlement where my mother lives.'

'You have my word on it,' said Prince Brian. He

turned away from the three and went swiftly across the grass, shouting, 'Patrick — Patrick....'

That very afternoon, Sunday or no Sunday, the work began on the boat.

'In the enclosure?' asked Prince Brian.

'No.' Ivar was scornful, sure of himself as never before. He's the one man who knows anything about boat-building, thought Emer, feeling proud of him. Everyone was looking at him with respect. 'No, by the river's edge — just there down in the Isle of Maain, where the forest comes to the edge of the river. Always build a boat near wood and water. We'll bring the tools down.'

Niall, Patrick's brother, was already going towards his workshed and sorting out adzes and spokeshaves and saws.

'Any iron needed?' asked Cormac.

'Thousands of nails, and when we've built the hull we'll need some brackets to fasten the crosspieces and the rowers' benches to the sides.'

'Get going, lad,' Cormac bawled at Flann, who had crept up to listen. 'At least you can do that. Pack all the nails you can get into that jar, and I'll start the fire going and make some more. There are plenty of axes, anyway. I made a lot of them to sell at the fair at Coad, and Niall put handles on them. Every man can have an axe.'

The whole troop of men moved merrily down to the riverside, and soon the air was filled with the sound of axes against wood.

Ivar and Conn were measuring out the space for the boat by the time Emer managed to escape from her mother and join them.

'Can I help?' she asked eagerly.

'No,' said Conn.

'Yes,' said Ivar, at the same moment.

They looked at each other and grinned. 'Well, she'll be useful,' said Ivar, a little apologetically. 'We're marking out a space for each man,' he went on, turning to Emer. 'You see, the rowers will sit in pairs, side by side, so we'll have ten rows for twenty men.'

'I see,' said Emer. 'So each little stick there shows where a rowers' bench will be.'

'Yes,' said Ivar. 'You go on marking the rowers' seats while Conn and I mark the outside.'

'Where do we put these logs?' asked Patrick, coming up with some short lengths of fir tree.

'Put them there, where the sticks are. They'll need to stand upright in pairs. They'll support the weight of the ship while we're building it.'

When she had finished, Emer wandered off to where Prince Brian was standing, looking thoughtfully up at a straight young oak.

'What are you thinking about?' she asked him, a little shyly.

Brian smiled down at her. 'I suppose I was saying a sort of prayer,' he said. 'You know, there was a time — long ago, before Ireland became Christian — when people worshipped oak trees. I was hoping that this oak might bring luck to our expedition to Limerick, and that we might manage to free Ireland of the Vikings.'

'Can I go with you when you go to Limerick?' asked Emer eagerly.

Brian laughed. 'Don't let your father hear you saying that,' he said. 'No, you stay here and have a big feast ready for us when we come back.'

'It's not fair,' said Emer. 'I'm only a year younger

than Conn, and he gets to do all the exciting things and I'm supposed to stay at home. I'm just as brave as he is.'

She watched resentfully as the men felled the oak tree and carried it over to the upright logs which stood ready to balance it. They began to shape it into a keel for the boat. Already she could imagine the boat, a large version of the little one Ivar had made on the afternoon when he had had the quarrel with Conn. She could imagine how it would sail down the River Fergus and into Limerick. If only she could go with them....

There had to be a way!

Chapter Ten

The work went on for another two months. Wafer-thin planks — strakes, as Ivar called them — were cut and shaped and nailed. There were ten for each side of the boat, perfectly matching and joined at the bows and the stern, each one overlapping the one beneath. Suddenly they made the boat take shape. Then the crosspieces were put in, each one exactly the right size to hold the sides apart, and the rowers' benches were placed above them.

'Looking for a job?' asked Patrick, as Emer came running down one day.

'Yes, please,' she said. She was never tired of doing things for this wonderful boat which was growing under Ivar's directions.

'Well, see if you can find Flann, and help him. He's picking moss. We need it to stuff in the gaps between the strakes. Ivar says that if you mix moss with sticky resin from pine trees, it keeps the water from coming into the boat. We need that moss now. I don't know what's happened to Flann; Cormac sent him off about half an hour ago, and he still hasn't come back. I would have thought even Flann would be able to pick a basket of moss.'

'Where did he go?' asked Emer, shading her eyes against the sun.

'Down there, beyond those oak trees.'

Emer nodded and ran off.

'Flann!' she shouted. 'Flann, where are you?'

She had gone quite a distance before she heard the familiar sound of Flann's sobs.

Oh, bother, she thought. There he was, no moss in the basket, lying on a heap of leaves and crying like a two-year-old.

'What's the matter?' she said impatiently.

Flann didn't answer; he just cried all the more.

Emer forced her voice to be more gentle. 'Is it Conn?' she asked, sitting beside him. Conn had been much better with Flann lately. He hadn't taken much notice of him, and he wasn't exactly kind to him, but all his energy was going into boat-building, and mostly he just ignored his cousin. Still, in an idle moment he was quite capable of teasing Flann, just to pass the time.

'Is it Conn?' she asked again. She rummaged in her pocket, found a scrap of linen, and gave it to Flann to wipe his face with. 'Go on, tell me,' she urged, trying to stop a note of impatience coming into her voice.

Flann sat up and shook his head.

'No,' he muttered. 'They're taking me with them to Limerick. Ivar said they should have a boy, some-one light, to sit in the bows and keep dipping a piece of lead into the water to make sure it's deep enough for the boat. He said he always used to do it when he was younger. So Father said that I should do it, and ... and ... I don't want to! I'm frightened — I don't want to see fighting and ... and blood....' Flann gave up the effort to speak and started to cry again.

So they're going to take this little scared runt and they laughed at the idea of taking me, thought Emer, boiling with fury and resentment. Why is being a boy so special, anyway? I'm worth fifty of him!

'I wouldn't worry,' she told him, stiffly and un-sympathetically. 'Your mother will never let you go.'

'Yes, she will!' howled Flann. 'They had a big row about it, she and Father, and in the end she said, "Have it your own way." I'll have to go.' He put his head down on the leaves and burst into hysterical sobs.

He even looks like a girl, thought Emer. In fact, he looks a lot like me.... Flann had the same black curls and blue eyes as his cousins, but he looked more like Emer than like Conn: his features were as fine as Emer's, and his body even slighter than hers.

Suddenly an idea came to her, and she caught her breath with excitement. Would it work?

She pulled Flann to his feet.

'Listen,' she said. 'Stop crying and listen. If you breathe a word about this to anyone, I'll kill you, but if you say nothing, you'll be quite safe.'

Flann caught his breath and made an effort. The wailing stopped, although tears still rolled down his face. He looked at Emer like a baby hare in a trap, and she suddenly found herself feeling really sorry for him.

'Listen,' she said gently. 'Don't worry. I'll take your place. They'll be going at night — I heard Prince Brian saying that; it will be dark. And we're about the same height. I'll wear your breeches and tunic, and your bratt, with the hood over my head. No one will know the difference.'

Flann looked at her with wide, startled eyes.

'Aren't you afraid?' he asked.

'No,' Emer said impatiently. 'It'll be great. I'd love to go.'

He was silent, but at least he had stopped crying.

A little colour had come back into his cheeks.

'Now wash your face in that stream over there,' Emer said in a motherly way. She felt so excited that she even wanted Flann to feel happier. 'Oh, good, there's plenty of moss on the bank. We'll have enough to fill the basket. You help me, like a good boy. Come on, let's stuff it as full as we can.'

She wanted to sing and dance and turn somersaults, but she forced herself to walk back sedately with Flann to the busy scene on the riverbank.

The boat's really looking good, she thought. Everyone was working on it: Conn and Ivar were seated on a bench in the bows, busily rubbing down their oars; Patrick was at the other end, fastening some crosspieces of wood to the stern; and Cormac was working on the mast, which lay on the bank.

Emer jumped lightly down into the boat and reached out a hand to Flann. 'Here we are,' she called out joyously. 'Flann has lots of moss, but he got himself lost.'

Cormac muttered something under his moustache and gave a glance of contempt at his son. Flann took no notice, however; he helped to stuff the moss into the sticky resin and then cram it between the strakes.

'I'll get some more; I know the way now,' he said happily, and ran off with the empty basket.

'Should I carve a dragon on the prow?' asked Niall. 'I can do it easily if you like.'

'Good idea,' said Patrick. 'We want it to look just like a Viking boat. What do you think, Ivar?'

Ivar nodded. 'Yes, a dragon would be good.'

'I've fitted some metal hooks to the mast, Ivar,' said Cormac. 'That means the sail can easily be lowered or raised with string.'

'Good,' said Ivar. 'We had no metalworkers in our settlement. This will be a better boat, much stronger, because of your work. The metal brackets will hold the crosspieces to the strakes very securely.'

'Look, Emer,' said Conn. 'This bench here is the one Ivar and I will row from. We're going to sit at the front of the boat, next to the prow, because we're the lightest. Father and Cormac are the heaviest, so they'll be at the back. Look at the holes in the side of the top strake; that's where our oars will come out. I've shaved them and rubbed them down until they're as smooth as silk. Feel them. See if you can find any roughness. Ivar says any roughness will slow down the rowing.'

Emer felt the oars. 'They're fine,' she said carelessly.

Then she lowered her voice. 'Where is Flann going to sit, Conn?' she asked.

Conn looked amused. 'Did he tell you that he's going? He's in a real state about it! We'll put some sort of box for him there in the prow. He doesn't weigh much — not much more than you, I'd say.'

That'll work out very well, thought Emer with satisfaction. If Conn and Ivar notice anything, they won't give me away, and the others will be further back. Father would be the most likely to notice, and he'll be at the back of the boat.

'Where will Prince Brian sit?' she asked.

'Oh, he's going to steer. He'll stand at the back, at the left-hand side, and hold the tiller — see, the sort of stick tied on with the piece of leather, over there.'

That's just perfect, thought Emer. Her high spirits were bubbling up inside her. She felt the oars and the oar-holes admiringly. 'They're wonderful, Conn,' she said. 'You're so clever to have learned to do it so well in such a short time.'

'Go on, curly-head, out of my way,' grunted Conn, but she could see that he was pleased at the praise.

She went down to the other end of the boat, to hold a piece of wood for her father. All the time, she could hardly keep the smile from twitching at the corners of her mouth. Limerick, she kept thinking. Adventure, excitement, Viking treasure!

~

Week after week, the work went on. Then, just one week before the festival of Christmas, came the splendid day when the boat was finally finished. Emer, with Flann at her heels like a well-behaved puppy, went flying back to the enclosure of Drumshee.

'Mother, Mother!' she yelled, as soon as she came within hearing distance. 'Deirdre, Orla, everyone — the boat is ready! We've been sent for the sail.'

Ita came out of the house, smiling a little at Emer's excitement, but quite excited herself. The other women also came out of their houses. This was the great moment. The sail, which they had so carefully woven and dyed with the roots of the madder plant, was about to be tried out on the boat which would take Brian Boru and his men on their raid against the Vikings of Limerick.

Flann ran to his mother and, catching her hand, snuggled against her. Quite gently, but firmly, Emer took his other hand.

'Come on, Flann,' she said. 'Help me carry the sail back.'

He came with her instantly, and she was pleased.

For the past few weeks, she had been trying to help Flann to grow up a little. The years of teasing which she and Conn had subjected him to had done him no good, she realised; but she found that if she gave him simple things to do and praised him, he seemed more confident. And the more he was kept away from his mother, the better. Deirdre treated him like a baby, and that made him feel like one.

'We'll all go with you,' said Ita. 'I'd like to see the boat on the water.'

'It'll probably sink,' said Deirdre sullenly. She was still furious about Cormac's insistence that Flann should go with them to Limerick.

Emer gave her an angry look. 'Of course it won't,' she said hotly. 'Ivar says it's the best boat he's ever seen.'

'Now stop answering back,' said Ita firmly. 'Here's the sail, then. Are you sure you can manage it? It's quite heavy.'

'I will if Flann helps,' said Emer, recovering her good temper. 'Flann's getting very strong — aren't you, Flann?'

Flann's colour rose, but a slight smile curved the corners of his mouth and he did his best with the heavy woollen sail, though Emer took three-quarters of its weight. Together they went down the Togher Field, towards the Isle of Maain and across to the riverbank. There was now a muddy path all the way, where Brian Boru's men had come and gone every day for the last few months. Soon they would be gone, and grass would cover the path again.

But before that, thought Emer, I'll have had the adventure of a lifetime. She beamed at Flann. I'll always be grateful for him, she thought.

However, once the sail was up and the boat was launched on the river, everything began to go wrong. The boat floated beautifully — it wasn't that; and the men all took their places and began to work the oars as if they had been trained to it from child-hood — it wasn't that either. It began to go wrong when Cormac called for Flann.

'We might as well take the lad now, to get him used to dipping the piece of lead and calling out when the water isn't deep enough. There isn't a lot of water in this part of the river, in any case. It would be a pity to run the boat aground on our first day.'

'No!' screamed Flann, his cheeks turning white. 'No, I'm not going. Emer promised!'

'Oh, no,' groaned Emer. 'You stupid little fool.' She took care to keep her voice down, though. Quickly she grabbed Flann's hand.

'It's all right, Flann,' she said, fighting to keep her temper under control and her voice low. 'It's all right, I'll come with you. We'll just pretend,' she added in a whisper. 'You'll be all right.'

Not waiting for a reply, she raised her voice. 'Father, I'll come with him. I'll show him what to do. Come on, Flann; we'll have to wade out to the boat. Don't worry — the water's very shallow here.'

There was another fuss while Flann wailed about his legs getting wet and his sandals sticking in the mud, but Emer kept a light grip on his arm and kept whispering promises in his ear, and eventually she got him on board. He was trembling all over. Emer gave Conn a fierce glance, which was enough to stifle the jokes on his lips, and took her place in the bows. She reached over to take the heavy lump of lead tied to a piece of rawhide the length of a man's stride.

'Tell him to sing out whenever the lead touches the bottom, Emer,' said Prince Brian.

'Wouldn't it be better if he just raises his hand?' asked Emer innocently. 'After all, you won't want too much shouting when you're going down the river at night.'

'Good thinking, Emer,' chuckled Prince Brian. 'I'll have to make you a general in my army.'

That was good thinking, thought Emer with satisfaction. If she kept her back turned and her hood over her head, on the night of the expedition to Limerick, there would be nothing to betray her — at least, not until light dawned in the morning; and by that stage they would have gone too far to turn back.

'Look, Flann,' she said, in the motherly tone that she always tried to use to him now, 'you hold that and just let it fall down. You can feel that the lead's still floating. So there's still enough water for the boat.'

Flann tried, holding the line as if it might bite him at any moment. Emer looked back. Cormac's face was a dark purple; he looked thoroughly ashamed of his son. Patrick was trying to keep a smile off his face, but Prince Brian was looking worried. He must have realised just how terrified Flann really was. At any moment he might suggest that they leave him behind and get either Conn or Ivar to do the job.

I must make it look like he can do it, thought Emer in a panic. She dropped the edge of her bratt over Flann's hand and, under its cover, took his hand in hers. What small hands he has for a boy, she thought. It's easy seen that he's never worked the way Conn's been working since he was five.

'Watch out here, Flann,' she said in a low voice. 'It could be getting shallow.' She remembered this stretch of the river; she and Conn had waded here sometimes, when they were catching trout. Only the very centre would be fit for the boat.

The lead bumped on the bottom.

'Quick,' Emer whispered. 'Raise your other hand.'

Flann held up his left hand limply, but it was enough. Every oar stopped instantly.

'Well done, Flann,' came Prince Brian's deep voice. 'Now make a cast over towards the centre, and wave us on if there's enough water.'

Under the cover of the bratt, Emer guided Flann's hand and nudged his other arm to make him raise it.

Let's hope this practice doesn't last too long, she prayed. I'll lose my patience if this goes on. He's like a limp rag.

Day after day they went out, practising their rowing, practising raising the sail; and day after day Emer sat beside Flann, a model of patience, and guided him into doing the right thing. And evening after evening she reassured him that he wouldn't have to go to Limerick.

'What's the matter with you?' asked Conn, one evening. 'You're not turning into a saint or anything, are you? What are you making such a fuss of that little rat for?'

'Well, if I don't help him, then you'll have to take his place,' said Emer. 'You know Ivar is a better rower than you, so if Flann doesn't go then you'll be the boy in the bows. How would you like that?'

That silenced Conn, as she had known it would. From then on, he and Ivar joined — rather insincerely — in praising and encouraging Flann; and Flann at least stopped crying and raised his arm whenever Emer nudged him.

After days of practice, Prince Brian called a meeting of all his men. They all gathered around the fire in Patrick's house. Emer kept in the shadows, but she listened intently.

'I know that you're all looking forward to the festival of Christmas,' Prince Brian said, his deep voice filling the little house. There was a movement among the men. They were indeed looking forward to Christmas, Emer knew; she had heard them discussing it. She looked at Brian Boru's determined face and began to guess what he had in mind.

'We won't be the only people planning for the winter festival,' he went on. 'The Vikings in Limerick will be drinking and carousing at Yuletide. For three or four days, they'll have nothing on their minds but having a good time.' He paused and then went on, 'And that's when we will fall on them and take back the treasure they stole from us.'

There was a moment's silence. Then every man in the place was on his feet, tankards of mead were raised, and the shout almost lifted the rafters off the little house:

'Brian *abú*!'

Chapter Eleven

Christmas Eve was a dull, damp, foggy day. The trees dripped with moisture as Brian Boru, his men, and all the women and children of Drumshee walked through the Isle of Maain and down to the riverbank. The fog was so thick that they could hardly see a foot ahead, and night was beginning to fall on this, one of the shortest days of the winter.

Emer was so excited that she could hardly keep from dancing along the path. The night before, she had gone over and over the plan with Flann, and even now she had to keep a sharp eye on him in case his nerves gave everything away. She turned back and peered through the mist; yes, there he was, hand in hand with his mother as usual.

'Flann,' she called, a sharp note in her voice, despite her efforts to keep her patience. 'Flann, come here. I want to show you something.'

He came, reluctantly, and Emer felt like slapping him. She had told him again and again that he was to stick by her, and then, when they got the chance, they would change clothes.

Now she had a bit of acting to do. 'Stay behind me, but quite near,' she whispered to Flann, as she ran on to join her mother.

'Mother,' she said to Ita, 'I think I'll go back to the house. I don't feel very well.'

'You seemed perfectly all right a minute ago,' said

Ita, her tone sharp and suspicious. 'You were skipping along like a young hare. What's come over you all of a sudden?'

Emer swallowed. It would never do to have her mother suspect that she was planning something.

'I just feel fed up that I'm not going,' she confessed. 'I know Conn is going to start teasing me, and I can't bear it.'

That was true enough, anyway. Conn's high spirits had been overflowing all the previous day; by the evening, even Ita had had enough of him and had sharply told him to behave himself or he wouldn't be allowed to go on the raiding expedition.

'Oh, all right,' said Ita, more gently. 'Never mind; they'll all be back in a couple of days, and then we'll prepare a great feast for Christmas. You can help me decorate the house, and the time will pass quickly. You go home. I'll be back soon. Don't lose your way in this fog. It'll be dark very soon.'

Emer nodded and turned to go back. She grabbed the startled Flann by the hand and pulled him behind a clump of young willows.

'Quick,' she whispered. 'Change clothes and then go back home.'

Flann made no move. Emer could feel him quivering all over as she struggled to take off his bratt.

'What's the matter now?' she asked, trying to keep the exasperation out of her voice.

'I'm scared,' muttered Flann. 'I'm scared that I'll be punished if anyone finds out.'

Emer sighed. They had been over that fifty times already.

'Your mother won't be cross when she finds you back in your house. She'll be quite pleased, really.

And your father will be well gone by then.'

'Will you come back to the house with me?' he whispered, allowing her to take his bratt.

'I can't,' she explained patiently. 'I have to be on the boat, or they'll start looking for you. Now give me your breeches and your tunic, like a good boy, and you put on my tunic.'

'It feels very long, your tunic,' Flann grumbled.

'You'll get used to it,' Emer answered shortly. 'No, go back that way. Hurry up, before it gets dark. Keep your head down and your hood over your face. But you won't meet anyone, anyway. They've all passed by now.'

Giving him a firm push, she turned her back on him. She had to trust him not to give her away, and do her best to play the part of Flann for the next few hours. Tightening her belt around the breeches, and letting the hood of the bratt fall over her face, she made her way through the bushes and came out on the riverbank just beyond where the boat was. Some of the men were already in the boat, and Ivar and Conn were fooling around on the bank, punching each other playfully.

'Now then, you two,' came Patrick's voice, 'calm down. We don't want two silly boys. We want two grown-up men.'

'Talking about boys, where's our hero Flann?' came Conn's voice, as Patrick waded through the water to take his place at the back of the boat.

This was an awkward moment. The real Flann would have spent a long time trying to get on the boat without getting wet, grumbling all the time. But, from the corner of her eye, Emer saw the shadowy figure of Deirdre move forward from the fog. She had no time to lose.

Quickly she jumped into the river, moved through the water as quietly as possible and took her place in the bows. She turned her face downstream and allowed the hood of the bratt to cover her face completely. With two exuberant splashes, Conn and Ivar climbed in behind her, emptying the water from their sandals over the side of the boat.

'All aboard?' said the deep voice of Brian Boru. 'Move off then, men, and remember: from now on, not a word unless it's necessary.'

'Flann?' came Deirdre's high voice. Is it just my imagination, or does she sound suspicious? thought Emer. She bent her head even lower, concentrating on letting the line with its lead weight trail through the water.

'Flann?' came Deirdre's voice again, and this time there was no doubt: she definitely sounded suspicious. Emer bowed her head and sent up a fervent prayer to the heavens.

'Be quiet, woman,' hissed Cormac. 'Didn't you hear what the prince said? No one must speak!'

The next moment, the boat was rocked by the force of a mighty stroke. Both Cormac and Patrick had pulled on their oars with all their strength. The boat surged forward. At this rate, they would soon be past Drumshee.

Emer began to breathe again. Luck was with her. She would soon be safe.

The boat went on, going faster than it had ever gone before. Concentrate, Emer said fiercely to herself as they rowed down the tree-fringed river. In this stretch of the river there were several shallow bits. She thought she knew them — she had nudged

Flann often enough, to make him indicate them —
but today the fog and the gathering darkness made
identification difficult.

The lead struck a rock. Swiftly she raised her arm,
and the rowing stopped instantly. Emer hauled up
the string and cast to the side. The water there
seemed deep enough; she cast again, to make sure,
and then motioned to the men. Swiftly the boat
pulled out and began to move downstream again,
going a little more slowly this time, to her relief.

They reached Ballycashin, where the River Fergus
went underground. This had been rehearsed again and
again. The men all leaped out of the boat; sticking
their oars through the rowlock holes, they carried the
boat over a mile of rough ground on their broad
shoulders.

Emer had known that this would be the danger
point for her, but in the event no one looked her
way. The mist was heavy, darkness had fallen, and
the task was hard enough to engage everyone's
attention. They stumbled over the hundred yards
and then thankfully launched the boat again.

Emer took her place in the bows and cast the lead
down. It floated. The boat moved off. Again and
again she tested, but they were coming into deeper
water. The Fergus had broadened out, and the boat
moved smoothly over it. If only some wind came up,
they would be able to sail. The men must be getting
tired, she thought.

Even as the thought passed through her mind, she
heard Conn falter and miss a stroke. He swore, and
Emer had a hard struggle to suppress a giggle. She
risked a quick look over her shoulder. Conn was
struggling to get his oar back under control. She

glanced at Ivar, who was leaning on his oar, waiting until Conn was ready; and suddenly she saw a look of recognition flash into his eyes. He knew who she was.

Quickly Emer put her finger to her lips, and Ivar nodded. She turned her head back, smiling to herself. She could hear the two boys picking up the stroke again. Ivar wouldn't betray her, she knew that. She could concentrate on sounding the depths of the fast-flowing river without worrying about discovery.

We must be past Quin's Lake now, she thought. The river had rounded a bend, and, although it was now quite dark, she sensed that they were going south.

Suddenly something pale flashed in the darkness. Emer only saw it for a moment, but she knew instantly what it was. It was the flash of a painted shield — a light-coloured painted shield on the side of a boat — in the middle of the river. A Viking boat was coming up the river, perhaps going to the settlement where Ivar lived.

She glanced back over her shoulder. All the men's backs were turned to her as they bent to the rhythm of the stroke. Only Prince Brian, with the tiller in his hand, was looking downstream, and his glance was fixed on the near bank. Emer was the only one who had seen the Viking boat; she had to warn them all.

She swallowed hard and found her courage.

'Prince Brian,' she said softly, wishing that she had thought of practising Flann's whining little voice. Instantly Conn's head swivelled around, and there was a startled exclamation from the stern of the boat.

Emer ignored them. 'There's a boat coming upstream. It's a Viking boat.'

'Pull to the left,' murmured Prince Brian. 'Pull in under those willows.'

The ancient willows hung over the river, their branches dipping into the water beneath. Swiftly the boat was rowed underneath; Patrick stepped ashore, a rope was flung to him and the boat was made fast to the gnarled trunk of a tree. They all held their breath.

There was no moon, no light from anywhere — and no wind. The sounds travelled clearly in the moisture-laden air: voices, speaking in a strange language. Emer heard Ivar draw in a quick breath, but he didn't stir. The noise of the Viking boat's oars seemed very loud. Emer strained her ears. They seemed to be going quite slowly. Of course, they were rowing upstream.

She was glad that the river went underground at Ballycashin. Otherwise she would have been frightened for Drumshee, with only Niall left to guard it. But the Vikings wouldn't find it. They had no way of knowing that the river rose from the underground cave only a hundred yards further on.

There was a shout from the Viking boat. Emer started with shock, sure that they had been seen, but Ivar reached over and took her hand in his, squeezing it reassuringly. She understood. He was telling her not to worry, that it was nothing. And, indeed, she could hear that the even rhythm of the oars hadn't changed. She squeezed Ivar's hand back, to tell him that she had understood his message; then she left her hand in his, feeling excited and thrilled by the whole adventure.

The sound of the oars was definitely getting fainter. The Viking boat was moving upstream.

'Another few minutes and we'll move off,' came Prince Brian's quiet voice. 'Undo the rope, Patrick; just hold it until we start to move.'

Patrick obeyed. Passing near the bows of the boat, he leaned over his daughter. 'Wait until I get you home,' he hissed.

Emer smiled to herself. Her father's bark was always worse than his bite. By the time they got home, she would be just part of the crew. They would all be so full of their success that her father would be in a great humour, and probably boasting about her to all the other men. In the meantime, she was safe, and soon she would be in Limerick.

Chapter Twelve

The night was still dark and misty when the River Fergus met another broad sweep of water. Brian Boru cautiously held up the covered lantern; then he bent over, dipped his hand in the water and licked his fingers.

'It's salt,' he said, a note of triumph in his quiet voice. 'We've met the Shannon. This is where the sea meets the Shannon and the Fergus. Turn to the left, lads. A good pull for half an hour and we'll be at Limerick. It's really an island between the Shannon and a river called the Abbey.'

They went on up the river, straining their eyes to see the lights of Limerick. Emer had nothing to do now — this river was both wide and deep — but she kept her eyes fixed ahead, and she was the first to see the distant light.

'There it is, my lord,' she said, keeping her voice low. 'There's Limerick.'

'That's it,' said Brian Boru, the excitement coming through his voice. 'That's Limerick. Now, when we get there, I want Ivar and Emer to stay with the boat. Ivar, I know you'd be a good man in a fight, but you can be more use if you stay in the boat. No one will question you when they see your hair and your looks. Keep the boat ready to cast off the minute we arrive.'

'What are our instructions when we arrive?' asked Patrick.

'No killing, if possible,' said Brian Boru curtly. 'We're here to get gold, silver, coins — anything we can carry safely. This is a raid, not a war. We can't fight the whole Viking settlement with twenty men. Keep under cover and keep quiet. Now pull, men, with all your strength. We want to get to Limerick before this weather lifts.'

As they came nearer to Limerick, the lights grew more numerous. By the side of the river they saw a bank covered with wooden planking, and several large iron hooks, fixed into the wall of the riverbank, ready for boats to be tied to them. Torches were fixed on iron posts above the bank, lighting up the whole quayside. There were four or five boats tied to the hooks, dark and empty and rocking slightly on the calm water of the river.

Brian Boru raised his hand and pointed, and the men pulled over towards an empty hook. In a moment the boat was secured to the hook and the men poured out.

This is great, thought Conn, moving up to take his place beside his father, at Prince Brian's left side. He had forgotten all the terror of the previous battle and remembered only the heart-throbbing excitement of it. He regretted that they weren't going to fight; his sword banged against his leg, almost inviting him to take it out and use it. But he knew that Brian Boru was right: there weren't enough of them to fight all the Vikings at Limerick.

The town — or longport — of Limerick was full of houses. Some were small houses like those at Ivar's settlement, made of woven hazel branches plastered with mud. Others were bigger, made from boards nailed together and thatched with straw. Others were huge, with big wooden roofs shaped rather like upturned Viking ships, and it was from these houses that most of the lights and sounds of merriment were coming.

Brian Boru stopped in front of the biggest one and cautiously put his eye to a window. Conn dived under his elbow, stood on tiptoe and peered in as well. There was a piece of oiled linen nailed over the window; but, with all the oil lamps and candles and torches burning inside, he could see everything as clearly as if he were in the room.

It was a huge hall, full of men. Along the sides were benches made of earth and piled with furs and sheepskins. Down the centre of the hall was a long table made of planks of wood nailed to trestles. The table, big as it was, was overflowing with food — great pies, succulent haunches of pork, chunks of roast ox, cauldrons of soup sending out mouth-watering clouds of meat-smelling steam. Fine white loaves of bread were piled high beside each plate, and great jugs of beer had been placed down the centre of the table. The Yuletide feast was at its height.

Conn swallowed, suddenly aware of how hungry he was, and looked at Prince Brian. Brian wasn't looking at the food, though. His eyes were fixed on the top of the great hall; and when Conn followed his gaze, he had difficulty in holding back a gasp of astonishment.

The end of the hall was heaped, almost to the ceiling, with treasure. There were saddles and bridles of the finest leather, helmets, gleaming mail shirts made from thousands of metal rings, piles of precious illuminated books. There were sacks of silver coins, chests filled to overflowing with silver and gold cups, brooches, necklaces, rings of gold and silver studded with priceless stones. There were heaps of furs, satins and silks, the firelight gleaming on the rare materials. Behind all the treasure was a small door, obviously a back way into the hall, as the great doors were at the other end.

Brian Boru moved away, and Conn followed him down to the other end of the great house. The main doors were open to the air, to let out the smells of cooking. Outside the doors were eight great torches made from pitch pine, flaring smokily in the moisture-laden air. Opposite the doors, only a few yards away, was a small building from which came clouds of steam.

Brian Boru signalled to his men to stay where they were, stole across the open space and peered in through the oiled-linen window of the smaller building. Conn couldn't resist the temptation: he darted after him. In any case, Prince Brian might need a messenger, he argued to himself. He stood on tiptoe and peered in.

The small house was crowded with naked Viking men, great burly men covered with hair — warriors, every one of them, thought Conn: their bodies were seamed all over with battle scars. At first he was puzzled, but then he remembered something Ivar had told him: Vikings often had baths — saunas, he had called them — in the middle of a feast, and then went back to eat more. These men were having a steam bath. The floor of the house was paved with flat stones; a huge fire burned in the centre of the room, and over it was a huge cauldron of boiling water, filling the small house with steam. As Conn watched, a man dipped a jug into the cauldron and poured water over the hot stones. The water bubbled and foamed, and clouds of steam rose up, almost obscuring their vision.

Conn looked at Brian Boru, who was nodding his head with satisfaction. Looking carefully around, the prince stole back to the waiting men, and Conn followed him.

'All men, except Patrick and Cormac, to the other end of this building,' Brian whispered. 'Cormac and Patrick will set fire to the steam-house. The men feasting in the hall will come out to put the fire out. When that happens, you must all burst open that small door, take as much as you can carry of their treasure, and run straight back to the boat. Take the small stuff. Go for the gold and silver. I'll stay here with Conn and send him to tell you when the hall is empty. Now remember, men: it's in and out, as fast as you can go. We'll only have a few minutes.'

The men moved away, silent as shadows in the murky air. Cormac and Patrick seized four torches each and went to the timber boards of the steam-house. They held each torch to a bottom board until it began to smoke, then moved on to the next board. Soon the steam-house was on fire, and shouts of alarm came from inside it.

Tense as a coiled spring, Conn watched until the first men burst out of the feasting hall, shouting over their shoulders for the others to follow.

'Now,' whispered Brian Boru.

In an instant Conn was gone. Brian Boru's men had already set their shoulders to the little door. One push and it crashed in.

The hall was empty, filled only with the smells of

food. Conn hesitated, giving a long glance at the table; then he resolutely grabbed a half-filled sack of gold coins and added a few gold cups, a gold necklace and a brooch. Beside him, Patrick and Cormac were doing the same thing.

'Quick,' said Brian Boru, entering the hall. 'Quick. Don't delay. They won't be long.'

Outside the hall they could hear shouts and orders and the confused noise of fifty men who had eaten and drunk too much and were now trying to put out a fire that was blazing out of control. I wish I could understand Viking language, thought Conn. We should have Ivar here. I suppose they'll have to get water from the river; maybe that's what they're shouting about.

He hoisted his filled sack onto his back and gave a quick glance around. None of the other men had left yet. He had a few minutes. Quickly he slipped down the hall to the table, snatched a large piece of pork pie and crammed it into his mouth.

'Greedy guts,' said a voice behind him. He whirled around and came face to face with Emer.

'What are you doing here?' he asked indistinctly, his mouth full of food.

She ignored him and ran up to the top of the hall.

'Prince Brian,' she called, 'Ivar sent me. He's had to move the boat. Follow me and I'll show you where he is.'

Chapter Thirteen

Emer felt terribly disappointed when the men climbed out of the boat and left her sitting there. She knew better than to argue with Prince Brian, though. No one ever argued with him.

She looked guiltily at Ivar. 'I'm sorry, Ivar,' she whispered. 'I suppose if I weren't here, you would have gone with the others.'

Ivar shook his silver head. 'No,' he said. 'It's best that I stay. It's a good plan. If anyone comes, I'll be able to speak their language; and if anything happens, I'll be able to move the boat. In any case....' He hesitated. 'In any case, I suppose Prince Brian thought that I might not want to kill Vikings, since I'm half-Viking myself.'

Emer said nothing. She wasn't sure what to say.

After a minute, Ivar continued, 'He needn't worry. I hate Vikings. I always have. My mother taught me to hate them.'

'Do you miss your mother?' asked Emer timidly.

Ivar shrugged. 'No. She doesn't want me. She told me that. She's better off without me. I was upset when she said that, but now I know it's true. My father never liked me, so I made trouble between them. I think she's begun to get fond of him, now that I'm out of the way.'

'It's a bit complicated, isn't it — with grown-ups, anyway?' said Emer. 'Flann's mother and father are a bit like that. They're always arguing, but I think they're quite good friends really.'

'In any case,' said Ivar firmly, 'I'm a man now; I'm nearly fifteen. Soon I would have married, and then I would have left my own family anyway.'

'Who would you have married?' asked Emer curiously. 'Was there a Viking girl you wanted to marry?'

'Well, there was one who my father wanted me to marry,' said Ivar casually. 'I didn't like her much. She was really stupid; she never had anything to say. And she wasn't a bit pretty. She had yellow hair in long plaits and a face like a cow.'

Emer smiled. She shook back her hood so that her black curls could be seen by the light of the torches at the quayside. She wondered whether Ivar thought she was pretty. I have plenty to say, anyway, she thought, and no one could say I look like a cow.

'I'd like to marry you, if your father would allow it,' said Ivar seriously. 'Would you like that?'

'Yes, I think so,' said Emer doubtfully. 'I'd like to live at Drumshee, though. I wouldn't like —'

She broke off. There was a noise from the river above them. She could see a moving light and hear the splash of oars.

'There's a boat coming,' she whispered, almost noiselessly.

Ivar nodded. 'Hide,' he said urgently. 'Get down under the seat and pull your cloak over your head so that you just look like a bundle. Don't move, no matter what happens.'

Emer did what she was told instantly. Maybe the boat will pass by, she thought. Maybe it's going downstream, down to the sea. It was coming nearer....

Suddenly an appalling cramp stabbed at her leg. She had it jammed into a space under the bench, and it was bent at an awkward angle. She had never imagined such pain. The only way to get rid of it, she knew, was to stand up and stamp on it. Could she risk it, or was the boat too near? She tried flexing her muscles without moving her leg, but it only seemed to make matters worse.

The next minute, she heard voices — strange voices, speaking a strange language. She knew she couldn't move now. She tried to remember everything Conn had told her about warriors who had endured torments of pain in battle. Surely she could endure the cramp in her leg. She tried to straighten it a little, without shifting her position, and clamped her teeth down on her lip.

There was another shout from the boat. It seemed to be almost on top of them; Emer could hear every drop of water falling from its oars.

Ivar answered, also in that strange language, his voice calm and unhurried. Emer felt a wave of pride in him. Yes, I'll marry him, she thought, and he and Conn and I will always be friends....

The voice from the boat called back. It sounded friendly, Emer decided; whatever Ivar had said, it must have reassured them.

Then she heard a bump. The boat had bumped against the wooden quay. That must mean that the Vikings were tying up their boat alongside Ivar's.

Panic filled her. When her father and Conn and Brian Boru came back, they would fall into a trap.

Ivar's voice came again. It sounded carefree, as if he was calling out some sort of greeting — or was it a farewell? The boat lurched a little, as if Ivar was pulling on the rope. Then something thudded into the bottom of the boat, just by Emer's feet. She stretched out her hand cautiously. It was a rope, still soaking wet from the river.

The next minute the boat lurched, tipping her off balance so that she lay sprawled on the bottom. Mercifully her face was still covered, so she made no attempt to move. She was just thankful that the sudden movement had released the cramp in her leg.

Ivar was rowing, not hurriedly, but strongly. They seemed to be moving out into the centre of the river. Wherever he was going, it hadn't aroused any suspicions among the Vikings: there was no stir, no noise from the other boat. Emer could hear the Vikings chatting merrily amongst themselves. They seemed to be unloading something from the boat. She heard the thumps of heavy objects on the wooden quay.

'You can sit up now,' said Ivar's voice, in Irish. 'Don't get up on the seat yet, but you can straighten up a bit. No one's looking this way.'

'What did they say to you?' whispered Emer.

'They asked who I was. I told them the truth: I said I was the son of Olaf, the boat-builder from the settlement on the Fergus. They assumed that my father was at the feast. They said they'd brought more beer for the feast. They stole it from the fort at Béal Borumha. They asked me to help them unload it, but I said I had to move the boat further upstream to pick up my father when he came out. They showed me where the feasting-hall is and said that I could get the boat quite near to it.'

'What are we going to do?' asked Emer trustfully.

'I'm going to moor the boat down here. I can see the roof of the feasting-hall. That'll be where they keep their treasure. If I stay with the boat, will you be able to tell Brian Boru where I am? You should be safe enough. It's only about a hundred paces away. You wouldn't be frightened to do that, would you?'

'No, of course not,' said Emer scornfully. 'Who do you think I am? Flann?'

And it's a good job that Flann didn't come, she thought with immense satisfaction. He would never have had the courage to do even something as simple as running a hundred paces up a Viking street.

'No one will see me,' she continued, in a lower voice. 'Even if they do, they'll just take me for a Viking boy, as long as I keep the hood of my bratt well over my face.'

'Be ready,' whispered Ivar. 'I'm pulling in. Do you see that roof — the one that looks like an upturned boat? That's the feasting-hall. Take care. Just have a quick peep around, and if there's no sign of them, come straight back here. Hold the rope. I've tied it to a ring on the quay.'

Emer sat up cautiously. There was no one around and she could no longer see the Viking boat, although she could still hear the thud of beer-casks being unloaded. She pulled her hood closely over her face and took hold of the rope. She and Conn had played innumerable games in trees with ropes, and she knew how to swing herself, with all her weight behind the swing. She landed on her feet on the quay and, without a backward glance at Ivar, set off running down the street, between the lit-up houses, towards the huge house with the roof like an up-turned boat — the feasting-hall, Ivar had called it.

There was something strange going on down

there, though. Emer could hear shouts and screams and yelled orders. Had they discovered Brian Boru and his men? She pushed herself to go even faster.

Then she saw great flames rising into the sky, lighting up all the dark houses. It's not the feasting-hall that's on fire, though, she thought. She could still see the roof of that. But other roofs, those made from thatch, had started to catch fire, and the shouts got even louder.

Suddenly a man came out of a nearby house. Before Emer realised what was happening, he had grabbed hold of her arm. Her heart almost stopped with terror, but then she noticed that he had an empty jug in his hand. He said something to her; he seemed to be asking a question. Maybe he wants to know if the extra beer has arrived, she thought.

She took a chance on it; she muttered something which sounded like a Viking word and pointed to the quay where they were unloading the casks of beer. The man nodded and laughed; releasing her arm, he set off down the street towards the quay without another glance at her.

Emer found that her knees were weak after the encounter, but she set off again resolutely, running as fast as she could towards the feasting-hall. The house on fire was just opposite it, but Emer ignored it and ran into the hall.

There was Conn — eating, as usual — and there was Prince Brian. She ran up to him.

'Ivar has had to move the boat,' she gasped. 'He's just down there. He says to come quickly.'

Prince Brian nodded. He said nothing, but he gave a quick, urgent whistle. All of the men gathered around him.

Emer turned to run out, and then stopped. On top of a pile of books was one which was familiar to her. It had a cover of purple vellum, bordered with paintings of flowers which grew in the meadows around Drumshee. Emer didn't need to read the gold letters on the cover to know what it was. She had seen this book hundreds of times, lying on the top shelf of the scriptorium, the writing-room, in the abbey of Kilfenora: it was the Psalter of King David, the abbey's prize possession.

She snatched it up and was out the door before the last of the men had joined Prince Brian. Pausing to make sure that they were all following her, she set off running down the street towards the river. There was no time to be lost. At any moment their presence would be discovered.

Emer was panting and she had a cruel stitch in her side, but she did her best to keep running. There seemed to be more smoke than flames coming from the burning house now. Soon the Vikings would come out and spot the strangers.

They came in sight of the river. Emer pointed at the boat where Ivar sat waiting. Brian Boru passed her, running strongly, all the men following him. Patrick picked Emer up as if she were a baby and set off after them, running down the boarded quay. How loud everyone's footsteps sound! thought Emer. Surely we'll be heard.... She looked over her father's shoulder. Conn was just behind them, a sack slung over his shoulder and another piece of pork pie in his hand. In a moment he had overtaken them and was climbing into the boat.

'Here, Conn, catch her,' whispered Patrick, throwing Emer down into the boat.

It was Ivar who caught her, however. He set her on Flann's box and took up the oars. Cormac, the last man to come, was climbing in.

'Pull, men,' said Brian Boru, and the men pulled strongly.

At that moment, there was a great shout from the town. The loss of the treasure had been discovered. Footsteps thundered on the boarded quay, and a shower of arrows rose into the air.

'Keep going!' said Brian Boru's voice. 'Row fast. We'll soon be out of range.'

'If we could just get some wind behind us....' said Ivar. 'Their boats are all just river-boats; none of them have sails. We must get out of range of their arrows.'

An arrow hit the bows of the boat, near Conn and Ivar. Conn leaned over and tried to pull it out.

'No, leave it,' said Ivar urgently. 'The wood will close around it; it won't do any harm. If you pull it out, you'll leave a hole.'

'Sorry,' said Conn. He still sounds excited, thought Emer. He had a sack of gold and silver at his feet, and he kept looking at it.

They pulled away from the lights of the town, out into the middle of the quiet, dark river. The arrows still kept coming, though, and they could hear feet thundering down the wooden walkways beside the river, keeping pace with the boat and even drawing ahead of it. There was a loud splash, as if a heavy body had fallen into the water; a few curses; and then, more ominous, the sound of oars in the water — not behind them, but ahead of them, barring their passage to the River Shannon.

'They've got the other boat, the boat that was bringing the beer,' said Ivar despairingly. 'It's no good — we're trapped. They're ahead of us.'

'Should we turn around and go back?' said Emer, looking over her shoulder. But even as she said it, she knew that it would be stupid to do that. The men on the walkways were still firing, and others were launching a boat from the quayside. They would be going into Viking territory, not escaping from it, and they would be easily trapped among the islands of the Shannon.

Another flight of arrows came hurtling over the water. There was a muttered curse from Patrick, and Emer saw his face screw into lines of pain. He was tugging at his leg. The shaft of an arrow was sticking out just above his knee.

In a second she was beside him, tearing off a piece of her linen under-tunic. He had managed to pull the arrow out, but the flesh of his leg was gaping open and the blood was welling out dangerously fast.

'Stay still,' Emer said through gritted teeth, pressing the wad of linen down on the wound so tightly that her arm ached. Half of the white cloth was instantly dyed scarlet with blood; but, to her relief, the top half stayed dry and white.

'I think it's stopping,' she whispered after a minute. 'Keep your hand on it, and I'll tear off another bit and bandage it over the top.'

'Doesn't make too much difference,' grunted her father. 'They're gaining on us from behind, and that other boat's ahead of us. We'll never get away.'

Emer looked around. The boat behind them had drawn so near that she could dimly see the faces inside the Viking helmets. The beer-carrying boat was being rowed — Ivar was right, neither boat had a mast for a sail, she noticed. It was making slow progress, but it was coming nearer. The men in it were shouting and waving sticks. They knew, now, that Ivar's boat wasn't a Viking one — that it held their enemies.

She turned to look at the boat behind them; and suddenly she realised that her face felt cool, and that her curls were blowing back from her face.

'Ivar!' she screamed, no longer worried about making a noise. 'Ivar, the wind's behind us. Raise the sail!'

Her cry was immediately taken up by Brian Boru. The men had practised this manoeuvre hundreds of times, and in a minute the great red sail was raised. The wind, strengthening every minute, filled it, and the boat sped on like a bird skimming the water.

There was a great shout from the beer-carrying boat. Clumsily it pulled across the river, positioning itself right in the pathway of the Irish boat.

Emer held her breath. She looked at the tall figure of Prince Brian, holding the tiller. Surely, if they kept going straight on, the two boats would collide and both would be wrecked....

The next moment she almost shot overboard as their boat lurched, not to the far side but to the near side of the river. Prince Brian was steering directly towards the bank, taking a chance that they were going so fast that the arrows from the men on the walkways wouldn't hit them.

The Vikings hadn't expected that; both boats had already begun to turn towards the far side of the river. A moment later there was a loud booming sound. Emer saw that the two Viking boats had crashed into each other, and most of the men were struggling in the water.

Prince Brian jerked the tiller again; this time Emer was ready and had braced herself firmly against the bows. The Irish boat turned towards the north-west. The south-east wind filled the great red sail, and they sped along so fast that the riverbanks began to blur in front of Emer's eyes.

The wind rose, and they went faster and faster. Emer could see the place where the River Fergus entered the Shannon. The danger was past.

The men rested on their oars and gave a great cheer. With this strong wind, they would be at Drumshee by morning.

'Have a piece of pork pie,' said Conn's voice. 'All this excitement is making me hungry.'

Chapter Fourteen

Christmas at Drumshee was all the better for having had to be postponed. Neither Conn nor Emer could remember ever having had such a good time. Gold coins were exchanged for goods and the best of food and drink, and there were presents for everyone. Conn gave his mother a gold necklace and Emer a gold brooch, from his share of what he had taken from the Viking hall. Ivar gave Emer a gold ring, as Brian Boru had insisted that he should have his share of the booty. Neither Ivar nor Emer told anyone else what the gold ring meant, but they went around smiling at each other for the whole of the festival.

At Emer's insistence, Conn gave Flann a present: some inks and brushes which had been inside a gold box he had snatched up at the last moment. Flann's great pleasure at the gift gave Emer an idea.

She had shown her parents the precious Psalter of King David which she had managed to rescue from the hall. On the sixth day after Christmas, she mounted her pony and rode over to the abbey of Kilfenora to return the book.

Abbot Finguirt almost wept when he saw his treasure returned to him unharmed. He poured out a torrent of questions and exclamations, and it was a long time before Emer could get around to the purpose of her visit.

Chapter Fourteen

'Father,' she said eventually, ruthlessly interrupting his account of the miracles of St Fachtnan and how the great saint must have protected the sacred book. 'Father, I want to talk to you about Flann.'

The abbot turned a puzzled glance on her. 'Flann?' he asked.

'Yes, Flann,' said Emer firmly. 'Remember when Conn and Flann and I used to come here for lessons? Flann was always the best of the three of us. He had the best handwriting — you remember that lovely copy of a psalm that he did? — and he was the best at Latin.'

'Yes,' agreed the abbot, looking interested. 'I was sorry when your parents decided that you and Conn had enough education and Flann stopped coming as well. Of course, Conn....' His voice trailed away. All the monks had suffered from Conn's high spirits. I don't think they miss *him*, thought Emer.

'Well, of course, Conn was really bored by book-learning,' she said briskly. 'And Mother and Father thought I had enough learning for a girl. But Flann would have liked to keep coming, only he was too scared to ride over on his own every day. But, Father, did you ever think that Flann would make a good monk? He's very gentle and he hates fighting, but he's always saying his prayers, and he would love to work here copying books.'

'Well, we would welcome him, if that is his wish,' said Abbot Finguirt eagerly.

It will be when I get talking to him, thought Emer. Aloud, she said, 'Would you talk to his father, to Cormac? Flann's very frightened of him, but you could make Cormac see that it's a great honour, and that Flann is really very clever in his own way. Cormac is ashamed of him, but that's because he sees that Flann will never make a good warrior, or a farmer, or a blacksmith. If Cormac thought that he might become a monk — an abbot, even — he would be proud of him. In any case....' Emer hesitated, and then went on bravely, 'In any case, I'm his only friend, and in another year I might be gone from Drumshee. I'm going to marry Ivar, the Viking boy, and he and I and Conn are all going to go with Prince Brian Boru.'

'But, Emer,' said the abbot, 'you can't marry a Viking! They are pagans!'

'Ivar wants to become a Christian,' said Emer briefly. 'I want you to instruct him, Father, and then he can be baptised and next year we'll be married. Will you come out to Drumshee this afternoon? Then everything can be fixed up.'

The abbot sighed, and then smiled. 'Still the same Emer, I see,' he said. 'You never could wait for anything, once you had your mind made up. Very well, then; I'll come out to Drumshee this afternoon. But tell me — will Ivar continue to live at Drumshee and work with your father and his brothers, or will he really join Prince Brian's warriors?'

'We'll go with Prince Brian,' said Emer, her face glowing at the thought of more adventures. 'He's promised that Ivar and Conn will be captains in his army.'

She glanced at the sun. 'I'll go home now, Father,' she said. 'I must talk to my mother and father. I'll tell Flann that you're coming.'

When Emer reached Drumshee, she found Ivar and Patrick standing together at the bottom of the path which led up to the enclosure. Ivar was very pale, and Patrick's face was flushed a dark red. Emer could read the pair of them like a book: Ivar had forced himself to talk to her father about the marriage, and now Patrick was angry. She would have to calm him down and make him see that it was a good idea.

'Ivar, would you find Flann for me?' she said. 'I need to talk to him, and I don't want Deirdre or Cormac to hear what I'm going to say. Bring him down here.'

Ivar shot off, his long legs covering the hundred and fifty paces uphill with effortless rapidity. Patrick gave a reluctant grin.

'You order that lad around like a slave,' he said. 'God help him if he marries you.'

Emer's heart gave a great bound of joy. It's not going to be too difficult after all, she thought.

She put her arms around her father and snuggled into his sheepskin jerkin. 'I love him so much,' she whispered.

Patrick patted her curls. 'Well, I suppose he's not a bad lad,' he said eventually. 'I don't know what your mother will say. You're too young to get married straight away, in any case.'

Emer nodded. 'Ivar has to become a Christian, anyway,' she said. 'We won't get married for at least another year. Ivar wants to earn his place in Prince Brian's army before the wedding, so he'll have money to keep me.'

'Well, I suppose we'll all be together, then,' said Patrick, becoming more cheerful by the minute. 'I'll be able to keep an eye on you if you're with Prince Brian; and your mother might come too, if her two chicks are going to be there. Prince Brian is talking about building a magnificent palace, so big that it'll have room for all his followers, over near the Shannon. He's going to call it Kincora. He was telling me about it the other night.'

'I know,' said Emer. 'I was listening. It sounds lovely — and it would be wonderful to be married to Ivar and still be able to see you and Mother every day.'

Patrick gave her a hug and a kiss. 'Do you want me to tell your mother?'

Emer stood on her toes and returned his kiss. 'You're the nicest father in the world,' she said. 'You tell her. I just want to give Flann a message, and then I'll be up to the house.'

Patrick set off up the path, still limping from the wound in his leg. Emer watched him lovingly. It was true: he was a great father to her. Her heart gave a great leap of excitement. Everything was working out.

'Father,' she called after him. 'Find Ivar, too, and tell him it's all right.'

He shook his head at her, and the word 'slave' came floating back down the path; but Emer wasn't looking at him any more. Flann was creeping down the Togher Field. His head was down and he looked miserable.

'Flann,' she said, taking his cold hands between her warm ones, 'Flann, walk down to the river with me. I want to talk to you.'

The whole way down to the river, Emer chatted about the abbey and about how happy Abbot Finguirt was to get back the Psalter of King David.

'He was saying how much he misses you,' she said innocently, with an eye on her cousin's face. 'He said you were the best copyist, for your age, that the abbey's ever known.'

A little colour came into Flann's face. His blue eyes darkened with pleasure.

'It was nice there, wasn't it, Flann?' Emer asked.

Flann nodded.

Oh, come on, Flann, say something, she thought impatiently. Aloud, she said, 'You liked going there, didn't you?'

Another nod.

'Do you wish you could still be there?'

Flann said nothing. I'll push him in the river in a minute, thought Emer, but she forced herself to keep a sweet smile on her face.

'Let's sit down,' she said, seating herself on a heather-covered rock and making room for Flann beside her. This is where Ivar and Conn had their boat-race, she thought. So much has happened since then that it feels as if it were years ago.

'Flann,' she said, 'what are you going to do when you're grown-up?'

He shrugged his shoulders.

'Are you going to be a farmer, or a blacksmith, or a wheelwright?' she persisted.

He said nothing, just stared into the fast-flowing River Fergus. His face had gone white again.

Emer took pity on him. 'Flann, I've got a brilliant idea,' she said eagerly. 'I've talked about it to Abbot Finguirt, and he thinks it's brilliant, too. Why don't you become a monk? You could spend your whole life at the abbey, copying books. They'd love to have you. Would you like that?'

Flann gasped as if she had hit him. Suddenly he stood up. His cheeks were blazing. Emer had never seen him look like that. He even looked taller.

'Would I be allowed?' he said, his voice not much louder than a whisper.

Emer stood up too. 'Let's walk down the road towards Kilfenora,' she said. 'Abbot Finguirt is coming out to see your father. It'll be all right.'

They walked down the road together until Emer's quick ear picked up the clip-clop of a mule's feet on the dusty road. She narrowed her eyes and satisfied herself that it was the stately figure of the abbot.

'You go ahead and talk to him,' she told Flann hurriedly. 'Tell him it's your dearest wish to join the monks. Don't be shy, now. Your future depends on it, remember.'

She gave him a little push down the road, then turned and ran back up the Togher Field and into the enclosure. Conn and Ivar were firing arrows, one after the other, into the straw target, shouting with laughter. Emer flashed a quick smile at Ivar. His eyes were very blue, and he looked very happy. Father must have spoken to him again, she thought. She didn't stop to talk, but went straight into the house to see her mother.

Ita was there, but so were Patrick and Prince Brian. Emer hovered in the doorway, suddenly shy and unsure of what to say. She looked at her mother, but Ita looked just as unsure.

Then Prince Brian stepped forward. 'She will be the most beautiful bride in the Kingdom of Thomand,' he said, and he bent down and kissed Emer on the cheek.

Patrick gave a proud laugh, and then Ita joined in, and in a minute everyone was hugging and laughing. Ivar was called in, and Conn was told the news.

'Poor old Ivar,' he said, and pulled Emer's curls.

Emer pulled his hair back, but not hard. She was brimming over with happiness; she felt as if she could never fight with anyone again.

'You'll have to find yourself a wife now, Conn,' she said. 'That is, if you can find anyone to —' She stopped. The dogs at the gateway had begun to bark.

'Someone's coming,' said Patrick. He limped to the door to look out.

'It's Abbot Finguirt,' he said over his shoulder. 'Flann's with him.'

Emer rushed outside, followed by Prince Brian and Ita and the two boys. Through the gate came the abbot, riding a white mule, and trotting beside him was Flann.

Emer ignored the abbot; while the others knelt for his blessing, she clutched Flann's hand. 'Well?' she whispered.

He nodded, smiling. 'Abbot Finguirt says I can join them immediately, if my father agrees.'

Cormac and Deirdre, and several of Prince Brian's men, had come out and were also kneeling for the abbot's blessing. Abbot Finguirt seldom left Kilfenora; only something of importance would bring him the four miles to Drumshee. There was complete silence when he began to speak.

'My son,' he said to Cormac, 'sometimes the Lord requires a sacrifice from us. To you and your wife, it may seem too great a sacrifice.' He paused, looking at their bewildered faces. 'Cormac and Deirdre, you have a very gifted son.'

From the corner of her eye, Emer could see Conn's face. He was staring at the abbot, and his astonished expression was so comic that she had to bite her lip to stop herself giggling.

Cormac looked almost as bewildered as Conn. 'Do you ... do you mean Flann?' he asked incredulously.

The abbot nodded. Deirdre moved towards Flann, shock and delight chasing each other across her dark, lined face. Very gently, Flann moved away from her and stood beside the white mule, his hand on the animal's neck.

'Yes,' said Abbot Finguirt firmly, 'I mean Flann. He is a gifted copyist and he would make a marvellous monk. He is a gentle boy, a good boy,' he added, with a glance at Conn's stunned face. 'It is his wish to join us, and we would be more than happy to have him. What do you say? You are his father.'

Cormac took one look at his wife. There were tears on her face, but they were tears of joy, and a proud smile was beginning at the corners of her lips. Then he looked at his son, and Emer held her breath.

Cormac had a curious look on his face; he looked as if he were seeing Flann for the first time. He put out his hand and patted the boy on the shoulder, then turned to the abbot.

'Father Abbot,' he said, 'we will be pleased and proud if you will allow our son to join the monks at Kilfenora.'

Deirdre gave a half-suppressed sob.

'Don't be sad, Deirdre,' said Prince Brian. 'This is a time of great happiness for us all. Flann will be a very good monk; we've won back spoils from the Vikings; and Emer and Ivar will be married.'

He turned to Ivar and shook his hand. 'Ivar, I wish you all the happiness in the world. I know you'll make Emer happy, and I thank you for all that you've done for me and for the Kingdom of Thomand. Your coming here has brought blessings to us all.'

'And you can all thank me for that,' said Conn smugly, with an eye on Emer's smiling face. 'After all, I'm the one who brought the Viking to Drumshee.'